THE GAME OF LOVE

"Cory, I need to talk to you for a minute." Clark's eyes were focused on the floor, but he kept her hand firmly in his. "I acted like a real jerk the other night. You had nothing to do with the team losing the game . . . I guess I've just been pretty uptight lately. I know it's a tall order, but do you think you can forgive me?" His eyes finally met hers. He looked so sad and vulnerable, Cory thought in a rush of affection.

"Oh, Clark," Cory cried, throwing her arms around his neck and giving him a huge hug. "Of course you're forgiven. I'm just sorry the whole thing happened at all—I was afraid you'd never speak to me again." They hugged each other tight. Cory felt the pain subside with each squeeze Clark gave her.

"I missed you a lot," he continued after a moment. "I hate fighting, and it was all my fault. Let's promise we'll never argue like that again."

"Never, never, *never!*" Cory replied, grinning. Before Cory knew it, her feet were off the ground and Clark was holding her in the air. She wanted to shout with joy. *We're back together*, she said to herself happily.

Bantam Sweet Dreams Romances
Ask your bookseller for the books you have missed

Sweet Dreams Specials

The Game of Love

Susan Gorman

BANTAM BOOKS

TORONTO · NEW YORK · LONDON · SYDNEY · AUCKLAND

RL 6, IL age 11 and up

THE GAME OF LOVE
A Bantam Book / October 1988

Sweet Dreams and its associated logo are registered trademarks of
Bantam Books, a division of Bantam Doubleday Dell Publishing
Group, Inc. Registered in U.S. Patent and Trademark Office
and elsewhere.

Cover photo by Pat Hill.

ISBN 0-553-27476-7

Published simultaneously in the United States and Canada

Bantam Books are published by Bantam Books, a division of Bantam
Doubleday Dell Publishing Group, Inc. Its trademark, consisting of the
words ''Bantam Books'' and the portrayal of a rooster, is Registered in
U.S. Patent and Trademark Office and in other countries. Marca
Registrada. Bantam Books, 666 Fifth Avenue, New York, New York 10103.

PRINTED IN THE UNITED STATES OF AMERICA

O   0 9 8 7 6 5 4 3 2 1

For my husband, Michael, whose encouragement, knowledge, support and love keep me going.

Chapter One

"Line set, 153, double G, on four," the quarterback commanded. Seven bodies on the front line tabulated their next move and repositioned for the play. Hearts beating with anticipation, muscles flexed, and concentration heightened, the two halfbacks and a fullback prepared to spring into action. "Hut one, hut two," shouted the quarterback. "Hut three." Hands positioned themselves under the center's legs. "Hut four." As the final call was made, each player jolted into action; the tackles and ends lunged forward, blocking the opposition. Halfbacks pushed forward, then fanned out, opening a gap between them. The guards kept the field clear, and the center lunged ahead and shifted suddenly to the right. As the quarterback calmly placed the football into the fullback's reliable hands, the right halfback carved a path through the hole that the others had made. Clutching the football, the fullback high-stepped away from a charging opponent and ran the last five yards into the end zone. TOUCHDOWN! A whistle blew, signifying the end of the play, and the offensive team shouted their success.

"That was perfect," the coach called through cupped hands. "Now let's see if we can do it just like that in the next game. Grab your gear. We'll meet by the bleachers to go over a few things."

It was a beautiful fall afternoon in Northbrook, Illinois. The grass still held its rich green color, but elm and oak branches danced with orange, red, and gold. The air was warm, but the oppressive humidity had disappeared. The breeze blew crisp and cool. Thoughts of cider, pumpkins, and sweaters replaced those of suntan oil, backyard barbecues, and T-shirts.

Football was the favorite topic of every male six and older. Would Glenview take the championship again, or had they lost too many seniors? Winnetka had already won their first three games and looked impressive. Football practice consumed dozens of hours during the week and was interrupted only by games on TV—and class attendance, which was mandatory.

This afternoon's practice was like any other in the North Shore suburb of Chicago—except for one thing. The players on the field were members of the Glenbrook High School girls' football team, the Powder Puff squad!

"That was a terrific touchdown you made, Cory," Beth Peterson said, blue eyes sparkling at her best friend.

"I was so excited when I completed the hand

off, I almost forgot to run," Cory said, laughing. "It's a good thing that Vicki is such a good quarterback. She could probably play every position and still win the game."

"Let's hustle, girls!" Clark Williams, the handsome senior who acted as coach for the Powder Puff squad, motioned the team toward the bleachers.

"You sure have a bossy boyfriend," Patti Miller, a tall, shapely girl, teased as she bopped Cory on the head.

"Hey, during football practice he's just the coach to me," Cory announced lightly. Cory and Beth picked up their pace and jogged ahead of the other girls. "I know they're just teasing," Cory whispered. "But I worry about the team thinking we get special treatment because we date the coaches."

"I know what you mean; Jon's only the assistant coach and they still give me weird glances when I get to run a play."

"Unfortunately, special treatment usually means that we get to stay after practice to pick up the equipment. I'll bet you a quarter we get asked to take the chalkboard in again," Cory said, grinning.

Cory and Beth sat in the second row of the bleachers with the rest of the fifteen-member team, and prepared to hear a lecture on keeping fit and getting enough rest over the weekend.

"You're looking pretty good out there," Clark said, pulling his blue Cubs baseball hat down to keep the sun out of his eyes. "But Jon and

I are concerned about the Puffs not having a game this week. Since Niles forfeited their game with us, we don't play again until we meet Lake Forest two weeks from today. I know we're undefeated after four games, but I think Lake Forest will be our toughest match yet."

"That's what he said about Des Plaines two weeks ago," Patti said quietly as she leaned over to Cory. "He thinks every team we play is the hardest to beat."

"Maybe that's because for *that* week, they are," Cory retorted.

"Girls, please try to keep quiet and pay attention." Clark glared at Cory, and she squirmed on the bench. *He's incredibly cute even when he's trying to be serious*, Cory thought, trying to suppress a smile.

"Sometime this weekend, I want each and every one of you to do a half-hour run." The girls all groaned. "C'mon, girls, where's your dedication? It'll make you feel great. Running builds up your stamina, gets your cardiovascular system going."

Cory started to daydream as Clark gave some notes and suggestions to the front line. She couldn't help smiling to herself as she watched him explain maneuvers. He loved football. It was one of the first things he had talked about when they started dating that summer.

The summer had gone by so quickly, Cory thought. There were so many things they had shared together. Picnics in the park, movies,

4

and evenings at the bicycle races. They had both worked at the Northbrook municipal swimming pool as lifeguards. She had noticed him the very first day. He was so tall and slender. His chest and shoulders were broader than a lot of the other senior guys', probably thanks to all the swimming he'd done over the years. Lots of people had remarked on what a cute couple they made. Maybe it was because Cory was athletic, too. She was petite but strong. She loved volleyball and tennis, and had once even thought about trying out for the gymnastic team—but "flag" football was becoming her first real competitive sport.

During the summer Clark and his best friend Jon Owens had tossed around the idea of forming a girls' squad. Cory had done some inquiring among her friends and found that there was a genuine interest in forming a girls' team. On the first day of school, she'd posted a sign-up sheet, and by the following Friday, there were twenty names on it. They'd lost five players in the first month, but the ones who had stuck with it were very devoted. Now they had the reputation as the only undefeated team in the league, and Cory and the other girls were very proud of the victories their hard work had won for them.

"Earth to Cory, Earth to Cory," Jon cried, snapping his fingers in front of her nose. "Clark wants me to have a chalk session about some new plays with the backs and ends."

"Sorry, I must have been daydreaming for a moment," Cory answered.

"About *football*, I hope," Jon scowled, resting his hands on the waist of his stocky frame. Then he laughed. A broad smile covered his freckled face as he ran his hand through his coarse, curly red hair. "Right now we have to go over these new plays."

"Sorry, coach," Patti's husky voice interrupted. "But it's after four, and if you want to get ready to play your varsity game tonight, you'd better get a move on."

"All right, all right, I guess that's enough for today. Everybody pick up the equipment, then hit the showers. Beth and Cory can take the chalkboard in." The two girls exchanged glances and rolled their eyes, remembering the bet they'd made earlier.

"I told you," Cory remarked, nudging Beth with her elbow.

"I don't believe it," Beth said, shaking her head. "This is the third day in a row we've had to lug this thing into the gym."

"I guess it's the privilege of dating the coaches."

The other team members pitched in and collected the balls, flag belts, and kicking tees while Cory and Beth struggled with the cumbersome chalkboard.

Cory smiled as they pushed the chalkboard through the leaves, thinking of last Saturday when she and Clark had raked leaves for her dad and then jumped and tumbled in the crispy piles. Then they raked them up again and cuddled up together to enjoy hot mugs of apple cider.

6

"Here, I'll get the sheet music and you take the piano," Clark teased, as he opened the wide double doors of the gymnasium, breaking Cory's daydream.

"Cute," Cory groaned as Beth headed for the locker room. "There's just one thing I want to know," she asked as she rolled the board into the corner of the gym.

"What's that, gorgeous?" Clark said as he pulled her behind the blackboard and gave her a quick kiss. Cory's heart skipped a beat as he held her tightly against his chest. The same sensation swept over her each time he touched her. She kept thinking it would diminish as they continued to date, but like magic, her body tingled at his touch, and her mind went blank except for thoughts of warmth and romance.

"Aren't you afraid that one of the other girls might see us?" Cory said, looking over her shoulder and catching her breath.

"The whistle has blown, Miss Hughes, the play is dead and the game is over."

"Looks like it's just getting started," Cory added, tickling Clark in the ribs.

"Hey, I call a foul. Now what was it that you wanted to know, anyway?"

Cory reached up on her tiptoes to put her arms around Clark's neck and stared into his misty gray eyes. He was so handsome, with his thick, wavy hair, sparkling eyes, and dimpled chin. Suddenly the chalkboard didn't matter anymore. The guy she adored had his arms around her and as far as she was concerned the world could melt away—she wouldn't even notice. "Oh," she said, rocking back and forth slightly. "I just wanted to know what time I should meet you before the game."

"Same time, same place, unless that's too early for you to get to the field?"

"No problem. I have to come early to set up the team's victory hoop, anyway."

"Ah, a pep club chairman's work is never done."

"You better be careful what you say," Cory chided, giving his side another jab. "Without a pep club, who would come cheer at your games?"

"Hey, Clark," Jon called from across the gym. "You about ready to go? I've got a lot of stuff to do before the big game tonight."

"Be right there," Clark said, slipping his arm around Cory's shoulder and walking out from behind their hiding place.

"Oh, I'm sorry," Jon said, turning bright crimson. "I didn't know you were, well, you know, busy."

"That's okay, good buddy, I was just explaining the intricacies of the quarterback sneak." Clark winked at Cory and she smiled, ruffling his sun-streaked, sandy brown hair.

She loved the way the sun played with those highlights. It made her think of summer days spent at the pool or the beach. Cory sighed. "See you later." She gave him a quick kiss on the cheek and headed for the locker room to take a shower.

"Getting a little extra coaching there, Cory?"

Patti's all-too-familiar gibing greeted her as she pushed open the heavy door to the locker room. Cory's mind filled with a thousand retorts, but she tried to remind herself that people like Patti weren't worth the effort. Patti just laughed and continued to blow-dry her curly mop.

"Sometimes that girl really gets to me," Cory muttered to Beth as she took out her towel and shampoo from her locker. "One of these days I'm going to let her have it."

"Yeah, get tough, Cory, that's the spirit," said Beth.

Cory looked at her best friend in silence, then burst out laughing. "Is this football talk, or what!" she said. "We'd better watch how much time we spend in the locker room."

"We're beginning to sound like real bruisers," agreed Beth. "Speaking of which, check this out!" Beth set her right foot up on the narrow wooden bench and rolled up her baggy pants leg. "Now tell me, how am I supposed to cover this up?" Beth's tanned skin couldn't hide the two-inch purple welt that covered her shin.

"That looks awful," Cory said, wincing, "How'd you get it?"

"It's just a reminder to me that I went out for football instead of ballet. I thought this was supposed to be called 'powder puff' football. I had no idea how hard a powder puff could be."

"I know what you mean." Cory grimaced. She ached all over after every practice.

The rest of the team had said their good-byes and left by the time Cory made it to the shower. Beth sat on a bench by the lockers, waiting for her.

"Sometimes I think the guys have it easier," Cory called over the hot, steamy water. "They're supposed to be tough."

"Yeah, that's for sure. The guys just mow their opponents down. They don't have to be graceful or cunning about it, the way we have to be," Beth agreed. "If we had to play that way, we'd be one big bruise from head to toe!"

"You're right." Cory turned off the water. "We should be happy that some genius invented makeup so we can cover up our bruises." Cory stepped out of the shower and wrapped a towel turban-style over her wet hair. "I'll jump into my jeans and fix my face and hair, then let's go get a bite to eat before we leave for the stadium."

"Are you meeting Clark at the first aid station before the game to give him his good-luck kiss?" Beth teased.

"How did you know about that?" Cory said, spinning around with surprise.

"I know everything you do, silly, that's what best friends are for."

"You're a spy, that's what you are." Cory grinned as she buttoned the top button of her jeans. Then she pulled the towel off her head and quickly snapped it in Beth's direction.

"Watch it, I'm already wounded!"

Cory pulled on her purple sweater and straightened its collar, then fluffed up her half-dried hair. "Let's go. I'm starved."

"See you both at the game," said a soft voice from the last row of lockers. Cory and Beth whirled around in the direction of the sound, startled; they had thought they were alone.

"Lisa, it's you," Cory exclaimed, plopping down on the bench.

"You scared me half to death," Beth quipped, leaning against the lockers.

"I'm sorry," the tall, slender girl said. "I just wanted to say goodbye." Her dimples deepened when she smiled. But Cory didn't trust that smile. Lisa just seemed *too* sweet. Lisa waved and hurried away.

"That was strange," Beth said. "I had no idea she was still here. I thought she left with the others. You know, I don't understand what she's doing on the team. She doesn't seem like the football type—she's so delicate."

"Talk about spies," Cory answered, picking up her denim jacket and tossing it over her shoulder. "She'd make a perfect one. She gives me the creeps."

Chapter Two

Cory leaned against the stucco building that was used as the stadium's first aid station. It was seven-fifteen and Clark was late again, but she was enjoying the quiet. It was the first time all day she hadn't been running around like a chicken with its head cut off.

There was a cool breeze that night and Cory was glad she'd decided to wear her pep club jacket. She glanced down at her uniform and crinkled her nose. This has got to be the ugliest outfit ever made, she thought. The skirt was forest green, lightweight wool. It had a kick pleat in the center of the back, which was inset with gold. Almost everyone wore a white button-down long-sleeved oxford blouse and white anklet socks, too. Cory wore baggy socks with her white sneakers because she thought they looked much cooler. To top off this horrendous outfit was a green cable-knit sweater vest with gold ribbing and the letter "G" for Glenbrook. Cory's "G" was different from most of the girls' because she was an officer in the club. The words, heavily embroidered at the bottom of the "G", signified her importance.

Right now Cory didn't feel very significant. Where was her boyfriend? Clark was really late, and if he didn't show up soon, she'd have to leave without giving him his good-luck kiss. She wasn't sure if their ritual worked, especially since the varsity football team had lost the last two games, but the kiss did wonders for *her* mood.

"Cory!" Clark's familiar voice called from the other side of the building. "Sorry to keep you waiting, but the coach went on for hours. I guess he's just trying to get us psyched up before we annihilate the other team." Clark slammed his fist into the palm of his other hand, emphasizing his determination.

"Sounds like another good coach I know," Cory said, crossing her arms across her chest.

"We've just got to beat Schaumburg tonight. Everybody's starting to get tense and insecure. When that happens we just don't work like a team, and we lose." Clark began pacing along the chain link fence that separated the stadium and the parking lot.

"Clark, it's all right. You're going to be great. All the injured guys are back this week, and you said you had really good practices after school. You've even got a number-one fan rooting you on, no matter what happens."

"Ah, Cory, you're the best," Clark whispered

as he stopped pacing. He took her left hand and gently kissed it before pulling her tightly to his chest. Wrapping his bulky arms around her body, he said, "I don't know what I'd do without you."

Cory could feel his heart beating through the bulky pads that covered his chest. She enjoyed being held like this more than anything in the world. She longed to tell Clark that she loved him. But in the three months since they'd started dating, he'd never said those three precious words. At first it had really bothered Cory. She had fallen for him so fast that she knew right away that she loved him. But most guys seemed different about that kind of stuff, so she resigned herself to the idea that Clark wasn't going to say "I love you" easily. But when he did, Cory knew it would be real and from the heart.

"You're just the best girlfriend a guy could ever ask for." Clark kissed the top of her head and then eased back to look into her blue-green eyes. "I've got to go now, wish me luck."

"Go get 'em, tiger!" Cory managed to get the words out though she was still daydreaming about their relationship. Clark lifted her chin with his hand. Slowly he bent down, and his warm lips met hers. They held the kiss for a moment . . . but it was over too soon. He gently brushed her light brown hair out of her eyes with his fingers before running off to join the rest of the team.

Cory stood motionless, still feeling the warmth of his lips against hers, his strong arms wrapped around her. Suddenly the breeze felt cooler, and she noticed the sky had turned a clear, dark blue. A crescent moon sliced the sky, and a few brave stars appeared. Cory sighed, pulling her jacket tighter around her. The laughter and shouts of band members filing off the bus into the stands brought her back to reality. "Time to wake up, Cinderella," she murmured, walking around the building to mingle with the rest of the crowd.

"That must have been some kiss," Beth teased when Cory returned to the stands. "I was getting worried. We've got a lot to do before the guys run through the victory hoop." Beth's voice lost its usual humor and an edge of panic crept into her tone. "Everybody has been asking me where you were. They want to know when they're supposed to go onto the field, and what cheers we're going to do."

"Okay, Beth, relax. I'll take over from here. I had no idea that running the pregame show for the football team was part of being the skit chairman, but I'm getting used to it. Thanks for holding down the fort while I was gone. I know how restless the natives can get."

"How's Clark doing?" Beth inquired, reverting back to her normal cheery state. "Jon's a mess. I made his favorite peanut butter cookies, and he couldn't even eat one."

"Did you ever stop to think that maybe it was your cooking?" Cory teased.

"Oh, you're just a bundle of laughs." Beth smirked, twirling a lock of hair. "Careful what you say, or you may just find yourself carrying that big metal hoop all by yourself."

"I take it back!" Cory pleaded. "You are the best chef in Chicago. Maybe the world."

"That's more like it," Beth said, picking up her pom-poms.

Glenbrook High School had two kinds of cheerleaders. First were the regular cheerleaders, the girls who could do flips, walkovers, and all types of splits. The other group were called Pom-Pom girls. They cheered at the games, waving their pom-poms, and did dance cheers at the pep assemblies. They were also part of the half-time entertainment at the games. The squad consisted of seven seniors and two juniors; each girl had a different letter to spell the Glenbrook name.

Cory had wanted to be a part of the Pom-Pom squad more than anything. Together with Beth, she had perfected a routine for auditions. Beth was chosen to be a Pom-Pom girl, but Cory didn't make it. At first Cory had been devastated when she wasn't chosen. As far as she was concerned, her whole high school popularity career had taken a serious nosedive. But the pep club had voted her into office the following week, and her confidence was renewed. She still wanted to be a Pom-Pom girl, but there was always next year, and as a senior she would have a better chance.

"Let's see if we can get some volunteers to help us carry this huge thing onto the field," Cory called as she walked over to the hoop.

"The freshmen did a really nice job painting the paper center," Beth added. The girls stepped back to admire the picture. The hoop itself looked like a six-foot metal Hula-Hoop. Butcher paper was spread across the middle and taped around the edges. In the center the freshman pep club members had painted a terrific victory scene. It showed the football team carrying coach Lang on their shoulders past the scoreboard, which read: Spartans 21, Wildcats 3. Around the edges of the hoop were green and gold crepe paper strips.

"Let's give a great big cheer for the freshman class," Cory cried to the group of girls who had gathered around to look at the painting. The pep club members cheered and applauded the class. The club's enthusiasm started to brew, and Patti, the head cheerleader, started everyone on the school song. By then a large crowd had gathered, and it was time to go onto the field and cheer the team through the hoop and on to victory.

"Okay, freshmen, you get to carry your hoop onto the field and we'll line up behind you and start the Fight Song. Onward, Spartans!" Cory screamed at the top of her lungs over the noise of the crowd.

"Great planning," Beth said to Cory as they started to jog onto the field. "Those freshmen are thrilled to be carrying the hoop."

"They should be," Cory agreed. "They did a great job on it, and they might as well flaunt it. Plus it just might show some of those snooty seniors that there are some students who still have pride in their school."

"Hey, Cory," Patti snapped, stopping Cory in her tracks. "I know you're in charge of pregame festivities, but don't think you can move in on my job and start dictating cheers."

"Sorry," Cory apologized as Patti rushed ahead to regain her power. "This is going to be a long year," Cory sighed.

"Don't let her get to you." Beth tugged Cory into position next to her.

"Where is everyone?" Patti called to Cory in between cheers. "Maybe the pep club chairman ought to do something about the small turnout."

"Ignore her," Beth said, loud enough for Patti to hear.

"Unfortunately, she's right. There are fewer people here this week than last. And about half as many as there were at the first game. What's wrong with this school?" said Cory, exasperated.

"Here comes the team," Beth shouted as the locker room door flew open and the players rushed onto the field. "I think I see Jon." Beth jumped up and down and cheered wildly, getting wrapped up in the excitement. The most valuable player from the previous game crashed through the center, tearing the carefully drawn artwork.

But Cory was still thinking about Patti's comment. Even though Patti was in a terrible mood and seemed to be taking it out on her, Cory knew Patti was right. She'd have to do something about the attendance soon. Just because the team was losing didn't mean that you were supposed to forget about it. That's when the team needed even more support.

"Look, there's Clark," Beth called, interrupting Cory's thoughts.

"Go, Number 84," Cory called, instantly leaping up and clapping. She blew him a kiss and said a little prayer. Keep him safe, and let him win.

Almost as quickly as the excitement had begun, it ended. The team had run through the hoop and were now stretching out and warming up on the field. The pep club gathered the hoop and rushed back through the team and into the stands, chanting, "Beat the Wildcats," as they ran. Cory and Beth stayed behind, picking up stray scraps of crepe paper.

"Well, your job's over for the rest of the night," Beth exclaimed. "Let's just hope we win so the rest of the evening is fun. Didn't the guys look terrific?"

"Ah, you fall for any man in a uniform," Cory joked.

"Just one crazy redhead. Look, I've got to get back. The squad's starting to get into formation. See you later."

"Okay. There are just a few pieces of crepe

paper left near the center that must've gotten tangled around one of the guy's ankles. I'll pick them up and catch you before the game starts." Beth joined her group and Cory jogged to the center of the field to pick up the few remaining streamers.

Both teams had finished their preliminaries. Cory hurried to clear away the paper. As she bent over, she spied something shiny about five feet in front of her. Cory swooped down and scooped up a coin, still jogging. This is great, she thought. Fifty cents will just be perfect for a nice cup of hot chocolate. But before she could pocket the money, she realized that she was not the only person running.

"Cory, stop!" Cory spun enough around to see an army of referees, football players, and officials chasing her. "What are you doing?" Clark barked, still jogging. "Drop it!" His voice sounded gruff and angry.

"What?" Stunned and shaken, Cory flung the coin back onto the grass.

"What was it?" the referee called. "Heads or tails?" Cory hesitated for a moment and bit her bottom lip as she realized she had ruined the coin toss. She glanced at Clark, who had his hands on his hips, looking angry. His teammates unsuccessfully tried to hide their laughter.

"Tails! I think it was tails," Cory blurted out. Both teams burst out laughing, and Clark hid his face as it began to redden with embarrassment. Not knowing what to say or where to look, Cory turned away from the howling team members and darted off the field. Before she could reach the sidelines, there was an announcement over the loudspeaker. "Due to a mishap on the field, there will be a retoss of the coin." Too embarrassed to face her friends' teasing, Cory rushed into the girls' bathroom and didn't come out again until the game was well under way.

Chapter Three

"I'm sorry about the game," Cory quietly said as Clark walked her up to the front door later that night.

"Which part?" Clark glumly asked. He stepped up onto the covered porch and leaned against one of the poles supporting the overhang.

"All of it," Cory managed to say as the lump in her throat began to tighten.

"I don't know which was worst: the fact that we lost the fourth game in a row, that I fumbled the ball twice on key plays, or that stupid stunt you pulled before the whole thing started." He turned away and crossed his arms tightly over his chest, staring down at the bushes that surrounded the patio.

"I said I was sorry. And it was hardly a 'stunt.' It's not as if I did it on purpose. If it messed up your concentration during the game, I apologize again." All evening Cory had held back her tears and emotions, knowing how Clark hated scenes. Suddenly the floodgates opened and she was crying, gasping for air. "I don't know what else I can say to make it better. All night you've blamed me for losing the game. You hardly spoke to me when we went out for pizza with Jon and Beth, and now you won't even hold my hand."

Before Clark had a chance to say anything, Cory turned the handle on the door and rushed in, slamming it behind her. Without pausing, she ran up the stairs that led to her room and threw herself onto her bed. She was crying so hard that she shook. A few moments later she heard the door of Clark's car slam and the motor whir as he peeled around the cul-de-sac at the end of the street. "Oh, Clark," she cried as she buried her head deeper into her pillow.

"Honey, are you all right?" Mrs. Hughes asked as she gently tapped on Cory's door.

"It's okay, Mom," Cory answered, wiping the corners of her eyes. "Clark and I just had our first fight."

"You want to talk about it, honey?"

"Not tonight, Mom." Cory choked on the last word as she started to cry again.

"Well, try and get some rest and maybe it won't look so bleak in the morning. I'll leave Puss and Boots in here with you to keep you company. Maybe they can make you feel better." Mrs. Hughes opened the door a little wider and the two family cats bounded into the room and onto Cory's bed.

Puss was a mischievous, golden-haired cat. She always seemed to be where she wasn't supposed to be, knocking things over and generally making a nuisance of herself. Boots, on the other hand, was much more dignified. He had large eyes, a beautiful amber coat, and two ivory "boots" on his hind legs that had earned him his name. Puss cuddled against Cory's ankles, and Boots nuzzled her arms. Cory took a deep breath and obliged them, finding a little comfort in their unconditional love.

"I wish boys were more like cats," Cory sniffed. "You wouldn't blame me for losing a dumb old football game, would you?" She snuggled closer to her pets, letting their purrs and the warmth of their furry bodies calm her frazzled nerves. Soon Cory was relaxed enough to try to sleep. She changed into a nightgown and crawled between the cool, fresh sheets. But her pillow was wet with tears. Silently she stared at the ceiling and went over the events of the evening again. *Why was Clark being so unfair?* she thought as a tear trickled down her face. And why was football more important to him than she was? Still heartbroken and confused, Cory drifted off to sleep.

On Saturday morning, Cory stared blankly at her image in the bathroom mirror. Her eyes were puffy and red, and her nose looked chapped. Her complexion, usually rosy and healthy, looked pale and blotchy. "Terrific," Cory grumbled. "I don't look *too* hopeless." The sarcasm rang in her voice. *I'm going to be totally transparent when I go to visit Gran this afternoon,* she thought. *She doesn't need to see me looking so depressed.* She splashed some cold water on her face and practiced some happy faces before she was ready to greet her parents at the breakfast table downstairs.

"Good morning, dear," Mrs. Hughes said, handing Cory a small glass of orange juice. "How are you feeling today?"

"Better, Mom, thanks," Cory said, forcing a smile. "I'm sorry if I woke you and Daddy when I came in last night."

"You know I never really fall asleep until you're home." She took a hot plate out of the upper oven and set it in front of Cory, who was sitting at the round kitchen table. "I fixed your favorite, French toast."

"That looks yummy! Thanks. Where's Daddy?" Cory asked.

"We had breakfast earlier. You know your father—as long as the weather's good, he and Mr. Denton try to play golf on Saturday so that Sunday's free for football."

"Oh, I don't care if I never hear that word again!" Cory sighed, pressing her hands against her temples.

"Which word?"

"Football," Cory groaned as she poured hot syrup over her French toast. "Is there anything you want me to take to Gran? I promised I'd stop by this afternoon."

"Maybe some Fig Newtons. You know how

25

much she loves them, but the nursing home cafeteria doesn't supply her habit." Cory and Mrs. Hughes chuckled at the thought of Gran smuggling cookies.

"I'll pick some up on the way," Cory said, finishing her last bite. "That was delicious, Mom, thanks."

"Maybe you can talk to her about your fight with Clark. She's pretty good about those things. Years of experience, you know."

"I'll think about it, Mom. I'd better take a shower and get going." She picked up her sticky plate, rinsed it, and deposited it in the dishwasher. "If Clark calls while I'm in the shower, let me know, okay?"

"I promise," Mrs. Hughes said, crossing her heart.

Twice during her shower, Cory turned off the water because she was sure she'd heard the phone ring. Each time, she anticipated their reconciliation. She imagined Clark begging for forgiveness, laden with flowers and candy. After all, he had some nerve, blaming her for his two fumbles. Unfortunately, by the time she had dried her hair and put on her makeup, he hadn't called. She procrastinated, trying on different outfits, hoping he'd call. After various combinations, she pulled on a dark red cotton turtleneck and then slipped into her camel-colored tweed jumper. Her ribbed tights matched the turtleneck perfectly. She slipped on her comfy loafers. Before going downstairs she checked the phones to be sure they hadn't been mysteriously disconnected. They hadn't. *Maybe I should call Beth and have her talk to Jon, who can talk to Clark, she thought. No, that's ridiculous. I'll have to work this one out all on my own.*

With nothing left to do, she gathered her purse and keys and headed for the car. "If anybody calls, tell them I'll be back no later than four," Cory instructed her mom before getting into the family station wagon.

She changed the dial to her favorite radio station, which was playing "How Will I Know if He Really Loves Me" by Whitney Houston. She felt as if a knife had been thrust between her rib cage. Her eyes filled with tears as the familiar melody took her back to the pool and the happy times she'd had with Clark all summer. *Were all their good times now a thing of the past?*

"That was from Lisa to her secret heart-throb," said the DJ. "And now we have an oldie but goodie, 'Breaking Up is Hard to Do.' "

Before the first chord hit, Cory switched the station. That station was also playing a song that reminded her of Clark. *Let's face it,* Cory said to herself, turning off the radio altogether. *Everything is going to remind me of Clark.* She tightened her grip on the steering wheel and decided to drive by his house on the way to see her grandmother. *If anyone is out front or in the yard, I'll just turn down the block before I pass the house. This way I can at least know if he's at home. Now I really am crazy,* she thought. *I've resorted to talking to myself!*

She made a right-hand turn down Walters Street until she could see the Williams' two-story house. Cory had a hard time telling if Clark's car was there because of the large elm trees in front of the house and the row of evergreens that lined the driveway. He drove a copper Nova that had been handed down to him from his older brother, Dave. Clark was proud of the car and spent hours tinkering with it when he wasn't busy waxing the exterior. Daydreaming, Cory recalled the fun-filled Sunday afternoon water fights they'd had over the car. How she wished that was the only kind of fight they'd ever have.

The blare from a car horn behind her jolted her back to reality. Suddenly she could see Clark lifting up the hood of his car. She quickly made a right-hand turn onto Church Street, swerving out of the way of a blue sports car and Clark's view. Horns honked angrily, and Cory pulled over to the side of the street to regain her composure. She rested her head on the steering wheel. "I have to get hold of myself!" she said out loud, trying to stop shaking. *Well, at least I know he's home,* she thought. *Maybe after a few hours of being a grease monkey, he'll calm down enough to apologize.* Confident that she was right, Cory stopped at a store and picked up her grandmother's treat on her way to the nursing home.

Lindhurst nursing home was about five miles from the Hughes' house. Cory's grandmother had decided to move there two years ago when failing health and the old family home had become too much for her. She hated leaving the house in Evanston where she'd lived for so many years, but as she put it, "When you can't even button your own blouse some mornings, it's time to pay someone who can." She didn't want to burden her daughter with all of her medical problems, so when the first offer came on the house, she sold it and moved into Lindhurst. It was an active community center where the tenants could enjoy everything from exercise classes to backgammon. Today Cory found her grandmother in the art studio working with watercolors.

"Gran," Cory said quietly as she tapped the tiny, gray-haired woman on the shoulder. "I didn't know we had a Picasso in the family. This is really pretty." Cory stepped next to the easel and admired the multicolored fall scene that was unfolding on the canvas.

"Oh, Corrine," her grandmother answered, somewhat startled. "I thought you were that snoopy old Janice, trying to steal my idea for her own painting."

"Why would she do a thing like that?" Cory asked, trying to hide a smile.

"Because she's got no talent of her own." Cory's grandmother set down her paintbrush and gently wiped her hands on a piece of cloth that dangled from her lime green smock. "I'm ready to stop for a while anyway—that last clump of trees on the right was created because my arthritis won't let me paint mountains."

"I think they look beautiful," Cory said, leading her grandmother by the arm toward her room. The halls were bright and cheery, lined with posters announcing activities and events that "the home" had scheduled. Several nurses greeted Cory before she and her grandmother reached room 127, where they sat down to have a chat.

"So what's new?" Cory asked cheerfully, setting the cookies on the nightstand.

"Absolutely nothing. I don't want to talk about me, I want to hear about your football team and that handsome beau of yours."

Cory sighed. "Well, football's great, Gran, I'm learning more every day. I'm just sorry I didn't get a chance to play it when I was younger. Have you ever played a sport?"

"The only thing I played, Corrine dear, was the violin and hooky."

Cory laughed and hugged her grandmother. "I can't believe you snuck out of school."

"I didn't sneak out, I just never showed up in the first place. Your grandfather was so embarrassed when the principal walked up to us at the café across from the school yard, I thought he'd call off the engagement right then and there."

"What do you mean?" Cory scooted to the front of her chair, dying of curiosity. She'd never heard this story before.

"Well, your grandfather was ten years older than I was, and he insisted that I finish high school before we got married. Little did he know that I had also applied to go to college.

Anyway, every Wednesday we met at Sheldon's café for lunch. I'd told him that I had the hour off from school and could meet him there. Well, that wasn't exactly true. I was so in love with that man I'd have said anything to spend a few hours with him. He never would have found out about my story if the principal hadn't figured out my scheme and followed me there." Cory's grandmother chuckled at the memory.

"What did the principal say when he saw you?" Cory asked, totally immersed in the tale.

"Mr. Hadley wanted to know what right your grandfather had to interrupt my very important education. Since your grandfather thought that everything was on the up-and-up, he was speechless. Everyone in the café was staring at us. Mr. Hadley took me promptly back to class and had a long discussion with your grandfather about my schedule. The meeting went on so long that Grandpa missed a very important appointment with a client."

"Did he ever talk to you again?" Cory asked, realizing the parallels to her own situation.

"Well, since we married a year later, had four beautiful children, and never spent a day apart, I think I can safely say that we worked through the situation."

"I meant how long did it take until he wasn't mad about it?"

"Men—and boys," Gran said, raising an eyebrow, sensing that the conversation had hit a nerve, "are very sensitive creatures. They don't like to have their feathers ruffled. Sometimes when things don't go exactly as planned they feel a need to blame someone else for their follies. After they blow off some steam, they realize that whatever the fight was about wasn't that important. You just have to be patient and wait for them to realize that."

Cory sat back in the chair and marveled at her grandmother's wisdom. For an eighty-seven-year-old, she sure was with it. "Patience? Are you sure that's all it takes?"

"It's harder than you think." Gran's brown eyes twinkled with knowledge, and her slender, bony fingers patted the top of Cory's hand. "If he really cares about you, you'll be able to work things through, and your misunderstanding will be a story you'll tell your granddaughter someday." She rested her hands back in her lap and gently smiled. "Enough of all this serious chatter," she suddenly burst out. "Let's break open those cookies!"

An hour later, Cory was driving home, evaluating the visit. She loved the fact that her grandmother called her by her given name, Corrine. It made her feel more sophisticated. And Gran could always cheer her up or help solve one of her problems. Leaving the nursing home was always difficult. Cory was never quite sure if it might be the last visit she'd have with her grandmother. She had so much love to give, and there was so much of life that Cory wanted to share with her grandmother. Cory couldn't bear the thought of missing one of their weekend visits. She made a promise to herself as she pulled into her driveway: "I will be patient," she said, "like Gran said. If he really loves me, this awful experience will be a tale we'll tell our grandchildren."

Chapter Four

"Coach Lang is looking for you," Beth said to Cory as she rushed up to their locker before first class on Monday.

"What for?" Cory asked. She pulled out her chemistry text and laid it on top of her heavy blue notebook. Cory examined Beth's flushed face and suddenly knew the answer. "He must still be angry about the coin incident on Friday." Cory slammed the locker door and clutched her books tightly across her chest. "I avoided him like the plague at the game."

"It wasn't your fault," Beth said sympathetically, trying to keep up with Cory's panicked pace.

"You don't think Clark told him to kick me out of the pep club?" Cory stopped dead in her tracks.

"Why would he do a thing like that? He's not still mad at you, is he?"

"He must be, I haven't talked to him since our big fight. He didn't call on Saturday, and he never called after I spoke with you on the

34

phone Sunday night." The girls gazed at each other solemnly. "If he did talk to the coach, we have a bigger problem than I ever imagined." Silently the girls walked the rest of the way to their chemistry class. Cory knew this was going to be one of those days.

"Coach Lang is looking for you," Patti leaned over to whisper just loud enough for the class to hear.

"Thanks, Patti. I'm not sure they heard you in the parking lot," Beth interrupted.

Mr. Nolan, the chemistry teacher, strolled into the lab, peering over his horn-rimmed glasses.

"Cory, Coach Lang has asked me to dismiss you a few minutes before class is over so that he can speak with you before gym class next hour," said Mr. Nolan. He did not look pleased about it.

Cory felt totally humiliated. She knew everyone was staring at her. The bottom of her stomach ached. Why hadn't she stayed home from school today? Because she was desperate to see Clark and clear up their problem before it blew itself out of proportion, that's why. She had come to school fifteen minutes early in the hope that he would be waiting at her locker, but no such luck. All weekend she'd thought about their fight on her porch, even though her grandmother had made her feel a little better. In her mind the events seemed to repeat themselves over and over again in slow motion. The scene would fade with the screech of his car wheels at the end of the block. But then she had visualized how they would make up. Clark would arrive at her house, begging for forgiveness. She would take him into her arms, they'd kiss, and all would be well. . . . But the weekend was over and they still weren't speaking.

Cory felt her stomach churn with nervous tension. What if he never came by to talk to her? What if they never got a chance to make up? How would she face him in the hall? What would she say if he didn't talk first? She just wanted to have the whole dreadful affair behind her. Now Coach Lang was going to chew her out. He might even ban her from football games for the season! Suddenly her head was pounding and the lump in her throat made it difficult to swallow. Tears stung at the back of her eyes. Without saying a word, Cory grabbed her books and purse and ran out of chemistry class. She was halfway to the bathroom before she realized she didn't have a hall pass, and the monitor was walking in her direction.

"Hold on a minute," the monitor called. "Oh, it's you, Cory. On your way to see Coach Lang, right?"

Cory couldn't take it any longer. She had been at school less than an hour and *everyone* knew what an idiot she'd been at the game and that the football coach was hot on her trail. She rushed into the girls' bathroom, snatching a handful of paper towels. She spent the next twenty minutes pacing the small room and trying not to cry. Every time she tried to calm herself down, she'd think of Clark, and the tears would start again. She tried to be positive about the situation, but she kept seeing herself standing outside the stadium watching all the girls cheer Clark on. Finally, at a quarter to nine, she took a deep breath and looked at herself in the mirror. Her eyes were red and puffy. "This is getting to be a habit," she said directly to her reflection. "Why did I pick up that stupid fifty cents? Well, what's done is done. Just face Coach Lang. Apologize for disrupting his game. That's all I can do. After all, I didn't mean to do anything wrong."

With that decision, and determined to shed no more tears, Cory marched into the hallway, down the stairs to the gym, and toward Coach Lang's office.

"Coach Lang?" Cory lightly tapped on his office door. "It's Cory Hughes." Cory heard some sort of commotion on the other side of the door. Feet shuffled and voices murmured.

"Come in," Coach Lang said in a stern voice.

Cory grasped the doorknob and took a deep breath. She opened the door, revealing a room full of coaches, assistant coaches, football captains, and co-captains—Clark was there, too. Their eyes met across the room for a moment, and Cory's mind raced with a thousand things she wanted to say. She looked down at the floor, embarrassed.

"I didn't mean to disrupt your meeting," she said meekly. "I'll wait outside until you're finished."

"No, no, Cory," Coach Lang explained. "We're all here to see you."

"You are?" she answered, trying not to stare at Clark.

"Oh, yes, we have something that we'd like to give you." Coach Lang stood up and came around his desk, positioning himself a foot in front of Cory. "On behalf of the coaching staff and the members of the Glenbrook Varsity and Junior Varsity football teams, we would like to present you with this plaque, as a remembrance." He held out a small rectangular plastic case, which had a Kennedy half-dollar sealed in the center. "Along with it is a document signed by each player and the staff, stating that if you ever need fifty cents, or a loan of any kind, you can get it from any of us, interest free, no questions asked. In other words, Cory, we'll be happy to give you our change, just don't take it off the field again." He winked kindly at her. "We just wanted you to know we're sorry we were so hard on you the other night. You gave us all a good laugh, once we got over losing the game." Before Cory had a chance to say anything, the group cheered and applauded, laughing at the folly that had appeared so grave only ten minutes earlier.

"I'm so relieved that's over!" Cory blurted, watching Clark's reaction. He was leaning against the wall near the back of the tiny room. His arms were crossed over his chest, but his face revealed that familiar cockeyed grin Cory had grown to love. Maybe he wasn't mad after all, Cory secretly hoped. But why didn't he call me? Didn't he realize how upset I was over this?

"There is one more thing," Coach Lang continued.

"Just don't kick me out of the games," Cory pleaded with a smile.

"Quite the opposite." The coach chuckled. "You're one of the best supporters we've got. What I would like to do is put in a request."

"A request?"

"The school is really down right now, because the team isn't winning. I was wondering if, as skit chairman, you could put together something to boost morale and present it at the pep assembly on Friday."

"Is that all?" Cory asked, still stunned that the imagined disaster hadn't materialized.

"That's a lot," Coach Lang stated, crossing to open the door. "All right, everybody, get back to class." Cory hesitated, watching Clark for a clue. Did he want to talk to her? He stayed in his place until Coach Lang and half of the guys had left and then stepped behind Cory, who was the last one in line. Only a step away from leaving the room, he took her hand and closed the door in front of her with his other hand.

"Cory, I need to talk to you for a minute."

Cory tried to evaluate his tone, to figure out what he was going to say next. His eyes were focused on the floor, but he kept her hand firmly in his. "I acted like a real jerk Friday. You had nothing to do with the team losing the game. I was responsible for my two fumbles, and I'm sorry about the way I acted at the pizza place, too. What happened before the game would have been funny at any other time, but I guess I was pretty uptight. I know it's a tall order, but do you think you can forgive me?" His eyes finally met hers. He looked so sad and vulnerable, Cory thought, in a rush of affection.

"Oh, Clark," Cory cried, throwing her arms around his neck and giving him a huge hug. "Of course you're forgiven. I'm just sorry the whole thing happened at all. I felt so bad about embarrassing you in front of your team-mates . . . I was afraid you'd never speak to me again." They hugged each other tight. Cory felt the pain subside with each squeeze Clark gave her.

"I missed you a lot," he continued after a moment. "I hate fighting, and it was all my fault. Let's promise we'll never argue like that again."

"Never, never, never," Cory replied, grinning from ear to ear. Clark stopped hugging her long enough to give her a long kiss. Then he pulled her tightly to his chest again. Before Cory knew it, her feet were off the ground and Clark was holding her in the air. She felt as light as a feather and wanted to shout with joy. Cory wished this moment would go on forever. As their lips parted, Clark twirled her around, laughing wickedly.

"Hey, what's going on here?" Jon's carrot-topped head peered into the coaches' quarters.

"Ah, gee, not again. Don't you two ever do anything else besides kiss and hug?" He covered his eyes and closed the door abruptly.

"That's all we're ever going to do from this time forward," Clark said, setting Cory down and beaming at her.

"Fine with me," Cory agreed, her eyes dancing.

"And if there's anything I can do to help you with the pep assembly, you let me know. I'm sure the guys on the squad would volunteer, too, as long as it doesn't cut into our practice time."

"Okay," Cory said, still too excited to think of anything but Clark. *I really blew this out of proportion, didn't I?* she thought. "Why don't we meet at lunch and see if we can figure something out?"

"I'll meet you at your locker, and we'll pick up where Jon interrupted us." Clark swooped Cory into his arms and kissed her quickly before he opened the door to walk her to the other side of the gym for her PE class. "See you in a few hours—don't forget about me." Clark bounded up the staircase and out the gymnasium's double doors. Cory looked after him, still in a daze. She wanted to pinch herself to make sure all the events of the last half hour were true. Actually, only one of them truly mattered. "We're back together," she said to herself, biting her bottom lip before breaking into a smile. Just an hour before, she hadn't been able to stop crying, and now her cheeks hurt from smiling so much.

*   *   *

"Hi, handsome," Cory teased as Clark greeted her at her locker before lunch.

"You're even prettier than you were two hours ago," he answered, stealing a quick kiss behind the opened locker door. "It's so gorgeous out, how about taking our lunches out on the side lawn. It's a lot quieter out there, and we might even get some privacy."

"Don't count on it," Beth announced, pulling open the locker to its fullest reach. "You're not the only couple trying to find a spot. Just because you're back together doesn't mean you get special privileges." Beth winked at Cory, who grinned back like the Cheshire cat. "I was just outside and it's like a sardine factory out there. I made Jon sit under the big elm and save us some places. He said he would if I'd bring him a double bacon cheeseburger for lunch."

"He's not going to be too thrilled when he finds out they're serving tuna melts in the cafeteria today," Cory said, putting her books away.

"Maybe I can get him a Snickers candy bar as a peace offering. He loves those things," Beth added.

"Plus I've got a great part for him in the skit I've planned for this week's pep assembly. Actually, I really need you both to help. I've got a great idea, but I can't do it alone," Cory said.

"That was quick," Clark remarked, looking a little surprised.

"I came up with it during English class."

"I'm sure your teacher appreciated that," Clark said, slipping his arm around Cory's waist.

"PDA, PDA," Patti Miller called from half-way down the hall. She was pointing at Clark and Cory. "I swear you two are the mushiest couple in school."

"Jealousy will get you nowhere," Cory cried in a singsong voice as the threesome sauntered down the corridor toward the lunchroom.

"Hey, did old power monger okay your skit for Friday?" Beth asked.

"I forgot all about her," Cory said, looking over her shoulder in Patti's direction. "She's going to want to know every detail before she gives us the fifteen minutes it's going to take to do it."

"Fifteen minutes! Wow, no skit has ever taken fifteen minutes before," Clark said before setting his tray on the serving shelf.

"Glenbrook's never been so down in the dumps before, either. I figure as long as Coach Lang has requested this skit, it had better have some effect on the student body or why waste the time. What I want to do is going to take longer than seven minutes, and if that means the cheerleaders have one less scream, then that's too bad."

"Whoa, get down, big thunder," Clark said, half amused. "You don't have to convince me, I'm on your side! But I'll bet you'll have to find a part in your presentation for Patti before she gives her approval." He picked up a

43

plate of tuna and set it on the tray with his scalloped potatoes, mixed vegetables, roll, and milk.

"If that's what it takes, that's what I'll do. This school needs to make up as much as we did, Clark, and if that means working with Big Mouth Miller, I'll do it."

Chapter Five

"Are you as scared as I am?" Cory asked Clark as they huddled quietly in the corridor listening to Coach Lang announce the skit that Friday afternoon.

"You know how I feel before a football game? Well, this is twice as nerve-racking. I don't know how Springsteen does it. I'm just glad this is a one-time event."

"Maybe I'll recruit you to do all my skits—then you can feel this way every week."

"No way," Clark answered, tickling Cory's ribs hard enough to make her yelp.

"Quiet," Patti ordered from the front of the line. "I can't hear my cue."

"Ignore her," Clark whispered to Cory before giving her a kiss.

Cory buried her head on his shoulder, inhaling deeply the scent of his cologne and soap. She loved the way he smelled. It reminded her of summer. The feel of cool water flowing over her skin, the scent of suntan oil in the air, a warm breeze ruffling her hair.

Those sensations were so strong, even now. Cory wondered if Clark ever had the same feelings when she was near.

"And now, the Glenbrook High School SNAP-RATS!" Coach Lang's voice pierced Cory's daydream and jolted the group into action. The school had no idea what was going to happen, and Cory crossed her fingers, praying that it would go as she hoped.

The group's entrance was welcomed with tepid applause and cheers. The eight-member cast opened the door and dawdled into their places as planned. Cory could feel her heart race with excitement and trepidation. It just had to work, she thought. There had to be something to jolt the students out of their apathy.

The cast lined up at the end of the gym under their school motto: All for one, and one for all. The crowd was still as Cory perused the stands. She squinted to look at the faces of her peers, all two thousand of them. They appeared uninvolved and lifeless. If her plan went well, she would soon look on the smiles of an involved, enthusiastic group.

Patti was first to step up to the microphone. She was dressed in a very expensive Esprit outfit. Everything was perfectly coordinated. The only thing unusual about her outfit was a large gold "S" pinned to the front of her sweater. Since she was usually peppy and loud, her first words to the assembly were somewhat shocking.

"I'm the 'S' in SNAPRATS, and I stand for

46

snob," she drawled. "If your clothes aren't perfect, I'll call you a slob." Patti strutted and posed for a few seconds before squealing, "For sure," and then walked down to the far left of the gymnasium.

Dressed as a photographer, Jon walked up to the microphone. He looked silly in white socks and too-short pants. He wore glasses that kept falling off his nose and had camera equipment hanging all over him.

"I'm the 'N' in SNAPRATS." His voice cracked with nervousness as he pointed to the gold "N" crumpled on his suit coat. "N for neg-a-tiv-ity. The only thing more negative than photographs, is me." He picked up one of the cameras and started flashing pictures of the floor and ceiling. Then he followed Patti and stood next to her at the other end of the gym.

Now it was Cory's turn. Suddenly she was petrified. There hadn't been a sound out of the student body. She didn't know if they were listening or if they were dead. Her feet felt glued to the floor, and she looked to Clark for encouragement. He was dressed as a real punker. Cory had spent half an hour getting his hair to spike. He was decked out in leather and chains and there was an unlit cigarette dangling from his mouth. He winked at her and smacked her on the shoulder, pushing her toward the microphone. Cory looked at him in shock and straightened her preppy outfit before starting her speech. She didn't realize he was taking his role so seriously.

"I'm the 'A' in SNAPRATS," she called, indicating the gold "A" on her sweater. "And I stand for apathetic. I don't know what that means . . ." Cory paused, looking bored, then shrugged. "And I really don't care." As she waltzed to her spot next to Jon, she announced: "When you're in student government, you don't have to care, you just have to be popular."

Clark was fast on her heels to center stage. "I'm the 'P' in SNAPRATS, and I stand for punk. I get bad grades, destroy property, and take lots of junk." He then took out an empty beer can and mimed popping a pill with the brew. He wiped his mouth on his green letter "P" and then swaggered over to stand next to Cory.

"Very convincing," Cory whispered out of the corner of her mouth. She was so proud of him. He had been reluctant to dress up and go in front of the school but had eventually relented when Cory had explained the importance of including all the types of kids who went to Glenbrook. Now she was worried she wouldn't get him off the stage!

Bryan, the good-looking senior class president, was next. He was wearing Clark's football uniform with a green letter "R" over the numbers. "I'm the 'R' in SNAPRATS, and I stand for rotten and rude. I push and I shove, I'm one scary, mean dude." He slapped his fist into his palm and then ran over to stand next to Clark, who growled at him when Bryan's shoulder nudged his.

Then came Lisa, the quiet girl on the Powder Puff squad. She had overheard Cory talking to Patti about the skit and asked if she could help. Since she was in the school choir, the band, and the drama club, Cory thought she'd make a perfect addition to the skit.

"I'm the 'A' in SNAPRATS, and I stand for atrocious." She was wearing Beth's Pom-Pom uniform with a green "A" attached to the front. "My attitude is awful, unpleasant, and precocious." She shook her pom-poms and joined the rest of the group.

Vicki, the girls' team quarterback, approached the microphone dressed like a stereotypical intellectual. "I'm the 'T' in SNAPRATS, and I stand for"—Vicki yawned—"tired. I'd rather sleep, I'd rather rest. I just can't get inspired." She slumped a little over her stack of books in front of her gold letter "T" and then slowly wandered over to her place in line.

The last member of the team was Beth. She was decked out in several different costumes from the theater department and carried a trumpet. Her green letter "S" was on a sash, and she modeled it for the audience to see. "I'm the 'S' in SNAPRATS, and I stand for spoiled rotten. If I don't get my way, I'd just rather be forgotten." She made a loud *blat* through the trumpet before joining the others.

For a moment the group continued to play their parts; each was looking to see if they had gotten the audience's attention or approval. No one was reacting to the events. Cory wasn't sure, but it was possible that her skit was turning into one big bomb. But failure or success, the skit must go on.

Cory nodded to Clark, who marched over to the microphone. Just as he was about to speak, suddenly all of the SNAPRATS pushed and shoved toward the microphone. It was a mess. The group formed a circle around the speaker and all crashed into each other, jumbling up their spelling before falling down. Serenely the actors lay on the floor for a moment before helping each other up in their new positions. Miraculously the letters all formed a new word: SPARTANS! Once again the members came to the microphone, but this time jogging with a new enthusiasm.

"I'm the 'S' in SPARTANS, and I stand for *sensitivity*," declared Patti.

"I'm the 'P' in SPARTANS, and I stand for *pride*," shouted Clark.

"I'm the 'A' in SPARTANS, and I stand for *action*," called Cory.

"I'm the 'R' in SPARTANS, and I stand for *reliability*," yelled Bryan.

"I'm the 'T' in SPARTANS, and I stand for *team work*," cried Vicki.

"I'm the 'A' in SPARTANS, and I stand for *achievement*," said Lisa.

"I'm the 'N' in SPARTANS, and I stand for *new ideas*," roared Jon.

"I'm the 'S' in SPARTANS, and I stand for *spirit*," cheered Beth.

Still jogging and full of energy, the group joined hands and started chanting, "All for one, and one for all . . ." over and over again. At first the audience just stared at them, dumbfounded. But then the cheerleaders and

Pom-Pom girls stood up and joined in, followed by the freshmen, the pep club, and the football team. That did it—finally, everyone was standing, cheering, shouting. Cory knew the message had gotten through, and elation mixed with sheer relief filled her. Someone, somewhere, started the school song. The band picked it up and soon the gym echoed with the sound of the entire student body singing the school song at the top of their lungs.

"It worked!" Cory shouted over the crowd to Clark.

"You bet it did," Clark replied with a grin. "I haven't seen this place look so excited since they declared the school lunches inedible."

"Great job," Beth cheered, full of excitement. "I have to admit I was a little scared for a while, but when I saw the punks stand up and cheer, I knew the message had gotten through." By now the cheerleaders had returned to their usual positions and were driving up the energy with newfound vigor. The members of the skit had faded to the sidelines to watch the crowd go wild. Cory was so happy she thought she might burst.

"J,J,JUN,I,I,IOR, JUN-IOR, YEAH JUNIORS!" The junior class started the battle of which class could scream the loudest. The seniors bellowed back, followed by the freshmen and the sophomores. Before they could start again, Clark tugged at Cory's hand and pulled her back into the corridor, where they had waited for their entrance.

"I'm so proud of you, Cory," he said, leaning her back against the cool tile wall. "Trying that idea took a lot of guts."

"Thanks," Cory answered quietly. She was pretty proud of herself. "I just hope the enthusiasm lasts longer than this afternoon."

"It will." He added, taking a step closer, "There's something else I want to last longer than this afternoon, or tomorrow, or next month. . . ."

"What's that?'" Cory questioned curiously.

"*Us.* I want us to last. It's been a wacky week, kiddo, and it's made me realize a lot of things. I really hated it when we fought, but it showed me something. That I don't want to lose you."

Cory's heart pounded with new excitement. She found it hard to catch her breath, and she was so touched and thrilled by Clark's declaration. "You won't lose me, Clark," Cory answered softly as she gazed into his dark eyes. "I won't let you."

"I was going to do this later, after the victory tonight, but I think this victory is good enough. Besides, I may not get a chance to be alone with you until late, and I can't wait that long."

"Wait for what?" Cory asked, unable to contain her excitement.

Clark reached into the pocket of his leather pants. He looked so different dressed the way he was that for a minute Cory looked at him curiously, as if she didn't know him. But when he spoke to her, his heart sang with the feelings they shared. Cory wouldn't care how he was dressed, it was who he was that had her so head over heels in love. "I want you to take this and wear it, so that every guy in this school, in this town, and in this state knows you're my girl." Carefully, he took Cory's left hand and slipped his class ring on her finger. "Will you go steady with me?"

Cory's skin tingled and she felt light-headed. Her hands felt clammy and hot all at the same time. She wanted to say, "I love you," and scream at the top of her lungs, but she couldn't do anything. For the first time in her life, she was speechless. She clutched Clark's hand, and her mouth dropped open.

"Does that mean yes?" Clark asked, somewhat unsure.

Still in shock, Cory just blinked to hold back the sudden prickle of tears behind her eyelids and nodded her head yes.

"All right," Clark cheered, swooping Cory off her feet. She hung onto his neck as he twirled her around, burying her head in his strong, broad shoulder.

"Yes, yes, yes, a thousand times yes!" Cory finally found her voice as he whirled her back into the crowded gym. She knew that the cheers were for the team, and the school, but right now she was celebrating her own private victory.

Chapter Six

"What's with you?" Beth queried Cory. "You're practically bouncing off the walls!" They were in the locker room changing into their Puff practice gear.

Cory didn't say a word, just held out her left hand for Beth to see the ring that was way too large for her finger.

"Oh, my gosh," Beth choked. "Is that Clark's?"

"No, it's Bozo the Clown's, dummy. Of course it's Clark's!"

"Oh, Cory, it's beautiful," she squealed, grabbing Cory's hand as she jumped up and down. The girls hugged each other and screamed with excitement. "When did he ask you? What did you say? Have you been keeping this a secret?"

"After the assembly today, yes, and no, I want the whole world to know," Cory answered in order.

"I can't believe it," Beth continued as she held her friend's hand and stared at the ring. "I mean, I can believe it, it's just that it's so sudden and wonderful, I think I'm going to cry." The girls hugged each other again, grinning from ear to ear.

"I'm still in shock," Cory said, shaking her head. "I can't stop smiling. This has got to be the best day of my entire life."

"What's all the screaming about?" Patti asked, walking over to the pair.

"Clark gave Cory his ring," Beth announced.

"He gave you an *engagement* ring?"

"No, no, of course not. He gave me his class ring. We're going steady," Cory answered proudly.

"How nice," Patti replied flatly. "I had one of those things once. It got caught on everything and I lost it six times." She turned around and walked out of the locker room.

"Now that's what I call a hopeless romantic," Cory said with a grimace. "Personally, I think it's beautiful, and I'm never going to take it off, so I can't lose it." She held out her hand and spun around, bumping into Lisa.

"Going steady, that's really nice," Lisa said, trying to step out of the way. "You're probably the luckiest girl in school."

"Thank you, Lisa, I think so."

"Clark's a great coach. I can imagine how wonderful he would be to date," Lisa added, blushing slightly.

"Okay, sports fans, let's hit the field! We've got a short practice today so let's make the most of it." Jon's voice blared over the locker room speaker.

"How are you going to keep that ring on

during practice?" Beth asked as the girls slipped on their sweatshirts and closed their locker doors.

"I'm not sure yet, but I can't take it off now, I just got it." She held her hand to her heart and squeezed it gently.

"Maybe we'll just go over plays, and you can keep it on. Then maybe you can get a chain to wear it on." The girls walked through the gym and out into the midafternoon sun. Closing her eyes, Cory lifted her face to the sun and took a deep breath of the clear, crisp air. What a perfect day to be in love, she thought. What a perfect day, period. The skit had revived the school's flagging spirit. Clark had asked her to go steady. Now, if the guys' team would only win tonight . . . Please let them win tonight, Cory silently prayed as she reached the track field where the girls' team practiced. She looked around but didn't see Clark anywhere. The rest of the girls had gathered center field, and Jon was about to blow his whistle to begin practice.

"Coach Lang has called an early meeting of the boys' team this afternoon," Jon announced seriously. "He's labeled it Operation Snaprat, thanks to Cory's inspiring assembly skit." The gang cheered and applauded, and Cory smiled and nodded her head in acknowledgment. "Personally, I don't think it would have had the same effect if I hadn't agreed to participate," Jon continued as he posed and bowed. The team laughed, and a few of the girls tossed sweatbands and towels at him. "All right, so what I'm saying is that Clark and I can't be here for practice. What we want you to do is a play check. Vicki will be in charge. She will call a play, and then ask one of you to define it." Half a dozen girls groaned before Jon could continue. "Keep it down. Then we want you to think up some plays of your own. You know enough now, so let's see what you can come up with. Okay, Vicki, you're in charge." The team turned their attention to their quarterback.

As he was leaving, Jon tapped Cory on the shoulder. "Can I talk to you for a minute?" Cory stood up and walked with Jon to the bleachers. "Clark asked me to tell you that he can't meet you before the game tonight."

"Is something wrong?" Cory asked quickly, somewhat concerned.

"Nah, he just thinks it's better if he stays with the team and concentrates on winning the game."

"Oh," Cory answered, a little disappointed. *He just gave me his ring, you'd think he'd want to be with me,* she thought. She had always thought her good-luck kiss was incentive, but since they hadn't been winning, she hoped Clark wasn't thinking she was a jinx.

"He said he'll meet you in the usual place after the game, and the four of us will go out for the biggest celebration Northbrook has ever seen."

Cory smiled, but she was sure Jon could sense her disappointment.

"I've got to go. Tell Beth the plan, and wish us luck."

"Sure thing," Cory agreed, giving Jon a light punch on the sleeve. She watched him run off for a moment before returning to the Puff squad. She felt as if her balloon were beginning to deflate but fought back the emotion when she glanced down at Clark's ring on her finger.

"Okay, Cory, your play is 116 MAN," Vicki commanded.

Cory thought for a minute, shifting gears into football mode. "That's the 100 formation, the 10 series means it's going to be a dive play, and the 6 indicates that the dive will happen by the halfback in the sixth hole on the right."

"Exactly. Beth, you're next."

Cory watched Jon jog across the field toward the gym. Her heart ached with a longing to see Clark. She desperately wanted to be with him. Now that they were going steady, all she could think of was spending more time with him. It was going to feel like years until they met after the game.

"Well, I think we're in pretty good shape as far as these plays go," Vicki said. "Let's try to dream up some new ones."

"I can hardly remember these crazy combinations. How am I going to think of one of my own?" Beth wondered glumly.

For about five minutes the girls tried to think up something creative. It seemed everything they came up with was just like the plays already on the roster.

"I don't think it's fair," Patti whined. "They want us to do their work for them. We can't be expected to be the coaches, too."

"I agree," Lisa said timidly. "I totally trust Clark's choices." She stopped herself and glanced at Cory. "Jon's, too."

"I don't think that's what the coaches are asking," Cory said, passing over Lisa's comment. "I think it's a vote of confidence for our team," she continued, trying to be positive and defend Clark at the same time.

"All right, then, *you* come up with something," Patti challenged.

Cory took a deep breath and looked at the squad staring blankly back at her. "What we need is a play that is so different that no team has ever tried it before."

"Great, what is it?" Beth chimed in.

Cory stood up and wiped her hands on the sides of her sweats. She paced back and forth, racking her brain for anything. "Maybe there's something girls can do that guys can't."

"That should be easy," Vicki teased. "I think there're lots of things girls can do that guys can't." The team laughed, and Cory was glad to have some of the pressure released. She looked out over the playing field and continued to think. As she scratched her head, she noticed the Junior Varsity cheerleaders practicing on the other side of the track. They were doing leaps, cartwheels, and jumps. Concentrate, she reminded herself. Then, suddenly, it came to her! "I've got it," she yelled. "It's very unconventional, but I think it just might work."

"What is it?" Beth asked, building enthusiasm.

"Well, you might think I'm crazy."

"We already think you're crazy," Patti said. "As long as it gets us a touchdown, who cares?"

"What is it?" Lisa asked as she stood up, eager to hear.

"Okay, everybody up on your feet and stand in formation," Cory instructed. "We'll call it 100 girls."

"What's that supposed to mean?" Vicki asked.

"Trust me, it'll make sense to us and confuse the opponents. When the center—that's you, Lisa—snaps the ball to Vicki, everybody do something."

"Do something?" Patti said, ready to abandon the plan.

"You know, like a cartwheel, or a roundoff, a stag leap, or just a jumping jack."

"You are crazy," Patti continued as she sat on the grass, disgusted.

"Now think about it," Cory said, trying to build confidence. "The other team will be so shocked that they won't have any idea what's going on, let alone where the ball is. So when Vicki gives me the hand-off, I'll be able to run the ball right down the middle before they have a chance to figure out what happened."

The girls laughed but agreed it might be worth a try.

"It's definitely unique, I'll give you that much," Beth said.

"I'm willing to give it a shot," Vicki called. "Let's try it on two." The team lined up as usual, giggling as they waited for the call. "One, zero, zero, hut one, hut two."

Lisa snapped the ball to Vicki, who handed the pigskin to Cory, who bolted through the center. She had a hard time keeping a straight face at the sight of arms and legs sprawling in all directions, but she made it through the uprights with one quick dash.

Half of the team stood up and cheered, and the other half were rolling on the ground. Cory raced back to the line of scrimmage for the verdict.

"We can only use this play if we know you're going to make a touchdown—and at the *end* of the game," Beth said, trying to catch her breath. She was sitting on the ground, holding her sides and laughing. "There's no way I can get up and concentrate on another play after this one."

"It may just work," Patti admitted, chuckling to herself as she bent over and grabbed the tops of her knees.

"There's only one problem," Vicki interjected.

"What's that?" Cory questioned, knowing that Vicki wouldn't pose any objections unless they were legitimate.

"I split my pants trying to do a cartwheel! I never was very good at those things." She grinned and turned around to reveal a long tear at the seat of her pants.

"And Lisa lost her sweatshirt. It flopped over her head," Beth added finally, gaining some control. "I guess we're going to have to tuck in our shirts before that particular play."

"Or charge admission," Cory teased.

"It's too bad that we don't have uniforms like the guys do, then we wouldn't have to worry about junk like that," Patti added, sitting on the grass.

"I've already ruined two pairs of pants," Lisa announced.

"You're right. It isn't fair that they supply the guys' team with uniforms. Why can't they do that for us?" Cory said.

"It's because the boys' teams charge admission and are a school-sponsored event," Beth replied. "We're just considered a club, so we have to have a money-making project if we need funds."

By now the girls had all gathered around the football and were listening to each other's comments about the injustices girls' sports teams suffered in high school.

"We're always treated like second-class citizens," Vicki stated.

"She's right; we're the undefeated team and we can barely get five people to come and cheer us on," Beth added.

"I just want to be sure I remember to tuck in my shirt before we do 100 girls," Lisa said, getting back to the original problem.

"Yeah, we'll need a sewing kit before we'll need a first aid kit," Cory joked.

"I think we should get uniforms," Beth insisted, taking a firm stand. "Mitch's Sporting Goods has tons of uniforms. Why don't we just buy some of those?"

"How exactly are we supposed to pay for them?" Patti fired back.

"Well, is anybody interested in buying a uniform on their own?" Cory asked.

"Isn't there some way we could make some money for the team to buy the uniforms?" Beth wondered.

"Sure," Cory said. "We can have a money-making project of some kind. But what?"

"The French Club earned enough money to go to France last year," volunteered Vicki.

"What did they sell?" Lisa asked.

"Magazine subscriptions. They made perfect Christmas presents."

"We don't have until Christmas, we need our uniforms now," Patti reminded them. "The Lake Forest team has gorgeous outfits, and they've had theirs all season."

"That settles it. I'm not playing another game until I have a uniform." Beth crossed her arms and pretended to pout.

"Well, in that case, we'll have to buy the uniforms now and have a money-making project later," Patti said.

"Or get a new halfback," Cory added, giving Beth a shove.

"I might be able to help," Lisa volunteered. "My uncle is Mitch of Mitch's Sporting Goods!

I'll talk to him and see if he'll let us have the uniforms for a small deposit and pay him after we earn the rest."

"Sounds perfect," said Patti. "Why don't you go call him now? Tell him he can come to all our games for free."

"They're already free," Beth remarked.

"He doesn't know that."

The team groaned at Patti. Lisa got up and headed for the phone in the gym.

"That still doesn't solve our money-making problem," Cory stated.

"We could wash cars," Vicki suggested.

"Or sell pennants," Beth added.

"What about singing telegrams?" Patti said.

"We need something fast, easy, and economical," Cory said as she pulled blades of grass out of the ground.

"You sound like an advertisement for a fast-food chain," Beth continued.

"Hey, how about a bake sale?" Patti suggested.

"Better yet, a pancake breakfast," added Cory. "I remember my brother's Boy Scout troop used to earn lots of money at those."

"Besides, the kids on the early buses are always complaining that they don't get to have breakfast because they have to get up at the crack of dawn to get here."

"Mary Ann Johnson is constantly saying that she's starved by the time she gets to school," Patti said. The other girls agreed and started to make plans for the event.

"We could do it on Wednesday, pick up our

new uniforms on Thursday, and wear them to the game on Friday," Cory suggested. "Pancakes aren't too expensive to make, and we could even buy some orange juice to sell with them."

"Even if each guy on the football team only bought one pancake for a quarter, we'd make something," Beth said.

"And what football player is going to eat just one pancake?" Vicki said, chuckling.

"Maybe we could set up a contest and have a prize for the person who eats the most," Cory said, caught up in the excitement. "I can see it now, Football flapjacks and O.J. Simpson Orange Juice."

The rest of the team cheered the idea, and the girls broke into committees to see who was going to do what. They were able to collect twenty-five dollars for ingredients and supplies, and Patti was put in charge of buying what they needed. Vicki would handle the advertisements and Beth and Cory were elected master chefs. The rest of the team would serve and clean up. By the time they had it all settled, Lisa came back with some news about the uniforms.

"We're in luck if we like purple and pink," Lisa announced, taking out the notepad she had jotted some notes on. "My uncle has an order that was supposed to be for a women's volleyball team, but they never picked it up. The shirts are pale pink with purple cuffs and collars and he says he can put our numbers on them as well. The pants are like sweatpants but they have some spandex in them, so they have a lot of stretch. The best part is that he has them in stock, and he'll throw in matching pink and purple striped socks for the grand total of eighteen dollars and seventy-five cents apiece. And if we put down half the price, we can pick them up before the game on Friday."

"I was kind of hoping for school colors," Vicki muttered. "I've never worn anything pink or purple."

"Then it's high time you did," Cory said, putting an arm around her shoulder. "I think it sounds perfect. There'll be no stopping the Puff squad now."

Cory kept twisting the ring around her finger as she headed back to the locker room. She couldn't believe what an incredible day it had been so far. The team was getting uniforms, the skit had been a huge success, but most importantly, she and Clark were going steady. She couldn't wait to hold him in her arms and give him a big congratulatory kiss after his victory that night.

Chapter Seven

"I'm exhausted," Beth said the following Wednesday morning as she poured another cup of pancake mix into the bowl. "It's seven AM and I feel like it's midnight."

"Just keep stirring," Cory said as she tossed eggshells into the garbage. "In less than two hours all of our hard work will have paid off. We won't have to paint another poster, flip a single flapjack, or wait on any more football players."

"What time did Clark say he was going to show up with the team?" Beth asked.

"Well, Jon was going to pick up half the guys in his folks' station wagon around seven. And Clark was borrowing Coach Lang's van to collect the rest of the squad. The way I figure it, we should have twenty-five hungry 'animals' converge on us around seven-thirty. I'm kind of surprised it hasn't started already. I've got all the bowls full of batter now—all we need is some customers." Cory wiped her forehead, leaving flecks of flour smudged on her face.

"Don't worry, the buses should be rolling up anytime, and we'll be swamped," Beth reassured her.

"I'm just a little nervous, especially since Clark wasn't that thrilled about this whole uniform thing anyway." Cory tested the griddle with a few drops of water. "All ready."

"I don't know why he'd think it would detract from the game. He could be upset because we're spending so much time trying to raise the money, but beyond that, I think it'll give us a new sense of pride. He should be glad that we have so much interest in our team." Beth seemed annoyed by Clark's complaints about the uniforms.

"You don't have to convince me," Cory said, turning up the hot water that was heating the syrup. "I haven't even told him about our secret gymnastics play, 100 girls. He seemed so unenthusiastic about the pancake breakfast that I figured we could spring the new play on him some other time." Cory frowned. Clark's negative response had taken some of the glow from her happiness on Friday. He'd seemed annoyed every time she brought up anything not having to do with his football game.

"Guys are weird sometimes," Beth added, taking out several tubs of butter from the refrigerator. "Some days they can be sweet and tender, and then other times they're more confusing than geometry." The girls looked at each other and laughed.

Cory knew she was right. She ladled batter

for the first pancake on the griddle and started daydreaming about all the times Clark had been sweet. She gazed down at her left hand, hypnotized by the light reflecting off the green stone in the center of his ring. Once again, she recalled the moment he had asked her to go steady. The twinkling of his eyes, the nervousness in his voice, but most of all, the tenderness of his kiss. She could feel her heart race every time she thought about it. The whole day had been perfect. And the guys' football team had finally broken their losing streak that Friday. The team had scored a tremendous victory, and Clark had made the first touchdown of the game. Cory had screamed so loud and hard that she practically lost her voice by the third quarter. But she had missed not seeing him before the game. The thought of losing even one chance to be close to him seemed unfair. She wanted to be with him all the time!

Their reunion after the match had been absolute heaven, though. Cory had waited outside the fence in the parking lot, their usual spot. As the minutes slowly passed, she watched all the other players emerge from the locker room to meet friends and girlfriends. Each time the door was flung open, her heart raced and her anticipation grew. She was so proud of Clark; she couldn't wait to show him how thrilled she was. Jon came out to meet Beth. Bryan emerged and came over to talk to Cory. Fifteen minutes more passed, and Cory was beginning to get nervous. Suddenly she felt strong arms wrap around her waist from behind. Lightly Clark kissed her on the neck, below her ear. Cory leaned her head back and let it rest on his shoulder. She closed her eyes and sighed deeply, filling her lungs with the fall air and the scent of Clark's cologne. Then, for a moment, she thought she smelled roses. And when she opened her eyes there were three of the most beautiful white sweetheart roses she'd ever seen, tied together with some baby's breath by a gold ribbon. The next thing she knew her lips met Clark's. She was in heaven again, and her love for him seemed to be all that mattered.

"Hey, Cory, we've got customers!" Patti's demanding voice shattered her daydream. "Coach Lang and the assistant principal are here for breakfast."

"Coming right up," Cory called back as she poured a cup of batter onto the griddle. "We're in business now."

For the next half hour Cory and Beth were nonstop flapjack flippers. Most of their customers were teachers. The first busload of early riders was late, and the football team hadn't shown, so there weren't as many customers at the start as the girls had hoped. It was a little discouraging.

"How's it going in here?" Mr. Miller, the principal asked, poking his head in the kitchen door. "The cooks said they'd let you use the facilities until eight, and it's a quarter to now. You'd better cook up the rest of that batter and then call it quits."

"But the football team hasn't gotten here for the contest yet," Cory replied.

"Well, we can't wait for them," he answered. "This is a school, not a restaurant, you know." With that he left the room.

"What could be keeping them?" Cory asked Beth.

"I haven't the foggiest notion. Maybe we should just make the rest of the pancakes and hope they show up soon."

"I'll tell Lisa and the cleanup crew to start clearing places so when they do arrive we can start the contest."

"If they don't make it, we'll have to award first place to Lumpy Phillips. He's eaten ten pancakes," Beth said. "He said he could've eaten more, but his mom made him have breakfast before he left the house."

"That's gross," Cory said, wrinkling her nose. "I don't think I'll be able to eat pancakes for at least a year after today."

"My compliments to the chef," Bryan's familiar friendly voice said as he carried in an armful of soggy paper plates. "Your Powder Puff team should earn quite a bundle."

"Thanks," Cory answered. "We're still waiting on the rest of the football team. They were supposed to be here a long time ago for the big contest. We really need the big eaters in order to buy those uniforms."

"I'll go see if I can find out what happened." Bryan tossed them a wave as he ducked out of the kitchen's swinging doors.

"He's so nice," Cory said to Beth as she

scraped the last of the batter into the sizzling pan.

"I think he likes you," Beth teased.

"No way, he's been dating Marcy Jacobson since the start of the school year."

"I heard that's only because you're seeing Clark."

"I don't think—"

"Sorry we're late," Jon said, bursting breathlessly into the kitchen. "The wagon had a flat, and it took us a while to fix it."

Beth cheered. "Well, here's a big fresh stack. Divvy it up among the team and we'll bring out the rest as soon as we can."

"It's just the five guys in my car. I don't know what's keeping Williams and the van. I figured they'd have been here long ago."

Cory turned over another set of pancakes. She didn't know whether to be angry or concerned. She couldn't believe that Clark had let her and the team down by being late. Especially when he knew how important this was to her. She tried not to imagine the worst, but she couldn't help worrying that Clark was in some kind of trouble. Had they had a wreck in the van? Her hands started to shake, and she burned her thumb on the griddle. "Yeow!" she cried as she jumped back, toppling the empty batter bowl onto the floor.

"Are you all right?" Bryan asked, rushing to her side. "Patti asked me to get the rest of the pancakes. Those football players are gobbling them up like hotcakes." The two of them laughed at the cliché, and Bryan set the bowl back on the counter. "Here, I'll clean this up. Beth can take out the last platter and you run your hand under some cold water. We can't have our star fullback injured."

Cory was too perplexed to protest. She turned on the faucet and winced as the cold water ran over her burn.

"Hey, Cory, have we got any more flapjacks in there?" Patti asked, rushing into the kitchen. "That scrawny little center, Jimmy Wilkenson, just polished off a dozen pancakes and is asking for more."

"The only thing left in here are the five burned ones from the first batch, and I don't think the birds are even going to want to pick at them. Mr. Miller made me stop making batter fifteen minutes ago."

"Well, I guess the contest is over then. The team will have to wash Jimmy's car sometime this week. We sure could have used that boyfriend of yours." Patti sighed, leaving the room.

Cory's concern had shifted to anger. Where was Clark? She knew he didn't think the girls needed to spend time trying to get uniforms, but Cory couldn't imagine him deliberately ruining their sale.

Lisa and Patti silently walked back into the kitchen, their arms laden with paper plates and syrup bottles. Cory averted her eyes. She knew it wasn't her fault that the sale hadn't been a complete success, but right now it sure felt that way.

"Vicki and some of the others are taking

down the posters. Is there anything I should do?" Beth asked as she emptied the trash.

"Protect my boyfriend from bodily harm," Cory muttered, rinsing out the dirty batter bowls. "Because if there isn't something seriously wrong, I'm going to kill him." She whirled around, brandishing a spatula.

"Take it easy," Beth said, stepping back from the sink.

"I'm just so frustrated and tired I can't think straight," Cory continued, resting her elbows on the counter and burying her face in her hands.

"Everything's going to be fine," Beth said, trying to comfort her friend. A loud crash disturbed the two and they both glanced at the door in time to see Clark's entrance. He looked rumpled, as if he'd slept in his clothes all night. His blue button-down shirt was half tucked in. He hadn't combed his hair, and you could still see the lines on his face from his pillow.

"Glad to see you could make it," Cory said sarcastically, turning her attention back toward the dishes.

"Oh, Cory, I'm so sorry," Clark apologized as he crossed toward the sink. "I don't know how it happened, but I overslept." He tried to slick his hair back and tucked in his shirttail. "I stayed up late watching some stupid movie, and when my alarm went off, I didn't hear it." There were a thousand words on Cory's lips, but she didn't dare say one of them. She had worked herself up into a frenzy and was trying really hard to keep from exploding. Instead she turned her head and glared at Clark.

Clark continued after a moment, "I didn't wake up until fifteen minutes ago when one of the guys called to see why I hadn't picked him up yet. I'm really sorry. . . . How'd it go?"

Just then Vicki and the rest of the team entered the kitchen. "Well, we made fifty-seven dollars and twenty-five cents," she announced. "Not bad, considering." For a moment everyone in the room stood motionless. Cory suspected that the team hadn't come in as much to make the announcement as to watch what would happen between Cory and Clark.

"Subtract the sixteen dollars and seventy-five cents for supplies, and it works out to be about two dollars and fifty cents per person," Vicki said, still tabulating.

Cory slammed down the ladle she was holding and started to march for the exit.

"I'm starved," Clark said, trying to lighten the mood. "I'll buy whatever you have left."

With all eyes on her, Cory stopped in the center of the room. Without saying a word she stalked over to the counter where the five burned pancakes still lay on the paper plate. She picked them up and thrust the dish at Clark before striding out the door.

Chapter Eight

"How could you embarrass me in front of everyone like that?" Clark demanded when he finally caught up with Cory in the hallway.

"How could *I* embarrass *you*?" Cory screamed, spinning around to face Clark.

"The whole thing was an accident."

"Are you sure about that?" Cory angrily continued. "You know what they say, there are no such things as accidents."

"You think I overslept on purpose?"

"I don't know, Clark. You weren't that thrilled about the idea in the first place. Maybe your subconscious just wouldn't let us succeed."

"That's ridiculous. It could've happened to anyone."

"Maybe so, but it happened to you and you're the coach of the Powder Puff team. You were responsible for getting twelve other guys here and you let us down. You let *me* down." Cory lowered her voice and stared at the floor.

"Jon messed up, too, and you're not blaming him."

"How can you even compare the two situations—and besides, we're not talking about Jon, we're talking about you. Jon was late because his car had a flat tire, not because he stayed up too late the night before." She started to walk to her first class, but Clark caught her wrist and stopped her. Cory tried to pull her arm away, but Clark held her firm in his grip.

"Look," Clark said calmly in a low voice. "The whole thing was unfortunate, and I'm sorry. I don't know what else you want me to say."

Cory closed her eyes and shook her head. "You could quit being so macho. Seems to me that sometimes you think the only things that are important are the things concerning you." She looked pointedly at her wrist clenched in Clark's grasp. "And then you could apologize to the Puff team."

"And what about you?" Clark asked, releasing her.

"If your apology to me is sincere, then it's accepted," Cory snapped.

"It sure doesn't look that way."

"Well, maybe I need a little time." With that Cory hugged her notebook to her chest and ran down the hall to her class.

Clark slammed his fist against a locker door, ignoring the stares from the kids in the hall. But when his hand began to throb, he regretted his outburst.

"Are you all right?" a quiet voice said. Someone lightly touched his shoulder.

"Oh, yeah, fine, Lisa," Clark said, rubbing the side of his hand.

"*I've* overslept a lot of times," she added sweetly. "It can cause a lot of problems."

"You can say that again!" Clark looked down the hall in time to see Cory slip into chemistry class.

"You'd better be careful with that hand," Lisa said, gently taking his hand in hers. "The school can't afford to lose its star player."

"Yeah, I guess you're right." He groaned. "Thanks, Lisa, you're very understanding." He looked back down the hall and grumbled, "Not like some girls I know."

The next few days were like a cold war between Cory and Clark. They weren't fighting, but a lot of the sparkle had gone out of their relationship. When they saw each other, it was casual, and their brief kisses weren't sending up any fireworks. Clark had apologized publicly to the girls' team and promised to help them in any other money-making ventures they came up with. Lisa's uncle Mitch had agreed to let them have the uniforms if they would pay in full by the end of the month.

On Friday afternoon in the locker room, a half hour before the big game, the girls' team was filled with a new excitement. Everyone was bustling before the big match with Lake Forest—everyone except Cory.

"Well, what do you think?" Beth said, twirling around to model the new uniform.

"I think you look great," Cory answered without emotion. Cory couldn't help but remember that these uniforms had caused the problem between her and Clark.

"Well, try to show a little more spirit then," Beth added, nudging Cory on the arm.

"I just hope we can play as good as we look. Maybe Clark was right when he said that uniforms will make us more concerned with how we look than how we play."

"Well, that's dumb. The guys wear uniforms. There's only one way to prove that he's wrong."

"What's that?"

"Go out there and beat those snobby girls from Lake Forest."

"You're right, Beth," Cory said, smiling. She slapped her thighs and jumped up to try on her new outfit.

The game was definitely the toughest the girls had played. The Lake Forest Lovelies were as serious about the match as the Glenbrook Powder Puffs. The first two quarters had been scoreless, and now in the third the Lovelies were within field goal range.

"They're going to try for a touchdown," Clark shouted from the sidelines.

"Keep your eye on the fullback," Jon added, running up the side of the field.

"Hold 'em!" the five girls on the Puff sidelines shouted.

Cory's muscles tensed. Her lungs tingled from the long run of the play before. She was a good player, but this game was really tough and was pushing her to her limits. Although each girl on the Powder Puffs played in every game, some only saw action for a few plays. The previous teams they'd played hadn't been that much of a challenge. But today, Cory had played both defense and offense from the start, and she was beginning to wear out. She hoped they'd win before her energy left her.

She lined up on the outside right-end position. As soon as the ball was snapped, she knew it was going to be up to her to stop the play. The halfback swept in her direction. Vicki grabbed for the halfback's flag, but it slipped away. It eluded Beth's grasp as well. Now it was Cory's turn. Her opponent was barely two feet in front of her and only ten yards from the goal line. Cory poured every ounce of strength into the chase. Twice she stretched her hand toward the elusive flag. Each time the wind whisked the flag just out of reach. She had one last chance—Cory hurled her body at the halfback, hoping to capture the flag. Cory's left shoulder slammed into the lanky girl's thigh. With her right hand she snatched the prized flag and tumbled with her opponent to the ground on the eight-yard line. Whistles blew and the play was officially dead. But the discussion between the referees and coaches was just beginning.

"It's illegal to tackle someone in this game," the Lake Forest coach argued.

"She was going for the flag and lost her balance," Jon defended. Silently, Cory waited for the outcome. To tell the truth, she wasn't sure what had happened. All she knew was that her head ached from a blow off the halfback's heel, and her new jersey was torn. The referee finally blew his whistle again and called the play legal.

"Since Number 44 had the flag in her possession, we must believe that her intention was to go for the flag and not the player." The Puffs cheered and the Lovelies groaned. Cory had prevented the touchdown. Unfortunately, the emotions were reversed minutes later when the Lovelies were on the scoreboard with a three-point field goal.

"All right, let's hustle," Clark yelled from the sidelines as he sent Vicki in with the next two plays. The first was a successful sweep for Patti on the right side for a gain of ten yards and another first down. The next play was stopped at the line of scrimmage by the large guard on the Lake Forest team. Short yardage was gained with a run by quarterback Vicki when she barreled her way through the center. It was third down and seven when Clark called for a pass play to Beth.

"My hands are so swollen that I don't think I can catch anything," Beth whined during the huddle. "Have Cory receive."

"You'll be great, Beth," Cory encouraged. "Remember, it's just like practice. We'll give you all the blocking you need, so take your time." As the team lined up in formation, it suddenly dawned on Cory that Clark had only given her two plays during the game so far. She had completed both with gains, but he was definitely excluding her.

"Three-eighty-seven rush, one," Vicki called out of the slot. The center snapped the ball a little high, but Vicki recovered quickly. She faded back, looking for Beth on the outside left. She took two steps before she could spot her downfield. Throwing with all her might, she watched the ball spiral through the air right on target. Then, as quickly as the play had begun, it was over. The sound of the leather slapping Beth's hands was almost deafening, as the ball bounced out of her hands and out of bounds. The whistle blew, and the Puffs returned to the huddle for their next play.

"Clark wants us to try it again on the right side," Patti sighed. The girls were silent as they looked at each other for reassurance.

"I can't do it," Beth practically cried. "I don't want to do it."

"All right, then, I say we try our secret weapon, 100 girls," Cory suggested. The teams' eyes lit up. "Does anyone have any objection to me carrying the ball? They won't expect it since I haven't touched it since the first quarter."

"Great," Patti said, giving Cory the go-ahead.

"Okay, everybody check their shirttails! Think of what you're going to do, and make it big," Cory said.

"One hundred girls on three," Vicki instructed before the team clapped their hands. Once again the Puffs lined up in formation. Cory's heart practically jumped out of her chest in excitement. Her legs felt like wet noodles. Vicki glanced at Cory and shouted, "One hundred girls, hut, hut, hut."

The play worked even better than it had in practice. The front line completed an assortment of gymnastic moves, including flips, walkovers, and jumping jacks. With very little effort, Cory grabbed the ball and dashed thirty-three yards for a touchdown. Then pandemonium hit! The team charged into the end zone to congratulate Cory. The referee could hardly blow the whistle because he was laughing so hard, but the play was a success. A few moments later the extra point was kicked by Patti, and the Puffs were ahead 7–3.

"Time out," Clark called to the referee. He turned around and sent Vicki back onto the field.

"Coach wants to see you, Cory," Vicki said proudly. "I told him that play had been your idea!"

"Let's hope he liked it," Cory answered, crossing her fingers before she darted to the sidelines.

"So you want to play coach, too?" Clark said flatly. "Hit the showers, Cory, it's over. You're out of the game. Lisa, take her place."

Lisa smiled and jumped up. "Anything you say, Clark."

Cory stood stunned for a moment, not knowing what to say. How could he be so unfair? Although it had been her suggestion, it had been a team decision to put in the new play. The coaches themselves had asked them to come up with new plays. Granted, with all the excitement over the uniforms, the team hadn't discussed it, but Cory didn't think she should be tossed out of the game. *Cory, it's over. . . .* This wasn't like Clark. Things had been shaky between them the last few days, but Cory had no idea he was going to take it so personally. Before she could say a word, he turned away from her, unwilling to hear an explanation.

"We're over," Cory shakily shouted, sliding the necklace that held his ring from around her neck. After throwing it into the grass, she ran to the locker room with tears streaming down her face.

Chapter Nine

Tears burned Cory's eyes as she ran toward the gym. She wanted to control her emotions, but every time she thought of Clark shouting, "It's over, you're out of the game," she sobbed even harder. She was beginning to regret doing something as rash as giving his ring back, but she felt terribly wounded. He had deliberately hurt her. First by not showing at the pancake breakfast, then by not letting her have any of her usual game plays, and now by completely throwing her out of the game without an explanation. She hit the bar to open the door to the gym and hoped that no one would notice her. Cory's stomach churned as she tried to hide her red face on the way to the locker room.

When she reached the locker room, she burst out weeping. She collapsed on a bench and buried her face in her hands. Already her sides hurt from crying so hard, but there was no stopping the tears. They seemed to have a will of their own.

"Cory, are you all right?" Miss Flory, the PE teacher, asked, poking her head out of her office. "Are you hurt? Do you want me to call the school nurse?"

"No, n-no, Miss Flory. I'm just—a little upset. I'm going to take a hot shower and then I'll be f-fine." Cory turned her back to the teacher and tried to sniff back the tears. Then she grabbed a towel off the stack at the end of the row and darted into one of the private showers. She tossed her torn jersey on the floor, kicked off her sneakers, and wadded the stretch pants onto the pile. The stream of water was strong and hot. But instead of comforting her, the water felt like little needles poking into her flesh. What had gone wrong, she wondered. Why should Clark be so upset about the 100 girls play? Although he usually called the plays from the side, Vicki occasionally altered one or two when she felt it might work better. Was he so egotistical that he couldn't have someone else stand in the spotlight? Or was it just Cory that made the difference? Was it because the team had rallied and bought uniforms? She couldn't believe that the boy she'd fallen so deeply in love with could truly be as self-centered as he now appeared. But why would he turn against her so vehemently? It was a nightmare.

Cory went through the motions of washing her hair and scrubbing the dirt from her elbows and hands. Everything kept whirling through her mind in painful detail. As she rinsed her hair, it really hit her. It's over, she thought. She and Clark were no longer a couple. She had tossed his ring onto the ground and called it quits. It meant no more long walks after practice, no more secret rendezvous before games. They wouldn't laugh at each other's stupid jokes over pizza. And most importantly, she would never feel his strong arms so securely wrapped around her or the touch of his soft lips against her own. A feeling of numbness engulfed her. She pressed her back against the wet tiles and lifted her face as warm tears mixed with the hot, pounding water from the shower. Her legs suddenly felt too limp to support her, and she slid down the wall and sat on the shower floor, letting the water pound on her head.

After a few minutes, Cory realized it was getting late. Surely the game would be over soon. She didn't want to talk to anyone, not even Beth. The thought of the team filing in soon, of having to deal with them, was more than she could bear. She had to get away quickly before they came back. Soon everyone would know of her humiliation, and she wasn't prepared to face them or their pity.

She peeked out of the shower to make sure that the locker room was empty. After toweling dry, she ran back to her locker, and pulled on her jean skirt and her navy sweater with the denim patches. It was one of Clark's favorites, and she had worn it especially for him that day. She shoved that thought right out of her mind and quickly slipped into her baggy socks and high-top sneakers. Any minute now she was sure the team was going to barge through the door and she wouldn't be able to make her escape. Dragging her jean jacket and purse, she flung her tote bag over her shoulder, hurried out of the locker room, and bolted up the long stairway. As she reached the top platform, the doors across the gym opened and the Powder Puffs filed into the building, shouting and cheering. Cory watched as Beth rushed ahead of the group. As Beth disappeared into the locker room, Cory ducked out of sight into the hallway by the cafeteria.

She would have to walk home, since she would ordinarily have gone out with Clark after the game and he would have driven her home. Beth had driven her to school, and she knew she could wait in the parking lot for her, but right now she didn't want to face anyone, not even her best friend.

It was a long, lonely walk home. She had a lot to think about, so she took an out-of-the-way route to ensure her solitude. Fall had definitely arrived. The daylight hours were growing shorter, and Cory felt the chill in the air. She slipped into her flannel-lined jean jacket and stuffed her hands in her pockets. She was glad it was Friday and she wouldn't have to go to school tomorrow. But what was she going to do about Saturday's football game? She didn't want to go to the game. She would play sick and find someone else to take over her pregame responsibilities. Tonight her folks were going to a supper club, so she could go into seclusion. But she would have to face her mother with some kind of explanation. Her mom hadn't been thrilled at the notion of Cory going steady. It sounded too serious for a girl in high school, she'd said. Now Cory would have to tell her it was more serious than she'd thought. They'd split up. And Cory had done the splitting. Her folks liked Clark. He was a good student, responsible and mature. Cory's dad said he brought out the sparkle in her eyes. What would he say when he saw her eyes now?

Cory walked along the fence of the swimming pool where she and Clark had met. The water had been drained after Labor Day, and all the lounge chairs were stacked in a corner covered with heavy tarps. The place looked as empty as she felt. Cory clutched the fence with both hands and closed her eyes. She remembered the time Clark had pulled a drowning little girl out of the water. She'd been so proud of him. He'd admitted later that he had been petrified, but somewhere deep inside himself he knew if he got her out of the water, she would be all right. Then she recalled the first time he had bought her an ice-cream cone at the concession stand. She'd teased him when he'd gotten ice cream on his nose. He'd gotten her back, though, by carrying her onto the diving board and dropping her into the pool, shorts, sneakers, visor, and all.

"I don't want to break up," she whispered to herself now as she leaned her forehead against the wire. But how was she supposed to deal with a guy whose ego seemed too big to include anything outside himself? She couldn't just stop being herself because she might step on his toes. Besides, he was the one who wasn't willing to listen to an explanation. But it was me who gave back the ring. Maybe we could still work things out, she thought, perking up for the first time in hours. I'll give him a call when I get home. He might even be waiting there for me. As long as we both want this to work, it can! Cory was suddenly filled with hope and determination as she remembered her grandmother's advice: patience. She had acted rashly, too, she thought, and if she didn't let her pride get in the way, within the hour they would be in each other's arms making up. And boy, did she love making up with Clark!

Cory jogged past the park and the elementary school with a lighter heart. From a distance she saw a car parked in her driveway, and her pulse accelerated at the thought of Clark waiting out in front. But as she got nearer she realized the car belonged to Beth.

"Are you all right?" Beth inquired when Cory reached the house, a little winded from running.

"I'll be better after I call Clark and we can talk things out. Come on in." Cory took out her key and unlocked the front door. Her mom was still at work, so the girls would have the house to themselves for at least an hour.

"Miss Flory said that you were crying and very upset."

"I was until about ten minutes ago when I realized that this whole thing was a misunderstanding and not the end of the world."

"I can't believe how you're reacting," Beth said as she slumped into one of the kitchen chairs. "I'd be an absolute wreck."

"Believe me, I was," Cory said, dialing Clark's number. "Shoot, it's busy; maybe he's trying to call me, too." She hung up the receiver and opened the refrigerator. "You want something to drink? I'm dying of thirst."

Beth just sat in the chair and nodded.

"So tell me about the rest of the game. Did we win?" Cory asked, popping open a cold soda and pouring it into a glass.

"Yeah, we won, barely. Let me tell you, it got worse after you left."

"Really? What happened? Was Clark as upset as I was?"

"Well, I don't know if that's the word I'd use, but he was definitely acting weird. Guess who he replaced you with?"

"Lisa, wasn't it?" Cory asked, glancing at the telephone.

"Yeah. She fumbled the ball twice, and the Lovelies made a touchdown off one of the fumbles. If Vicki hadn't stopped the runner on the two-point conversion, we would've lost. As it was, we only won by one point."

"I wonder why he put Lisa in. I mean, she's fine as a center every once in a while, but even she'll admit that she's petrified to touch the ball." Cory jumped up again and began dialing Clark's number. "Still busy," she sighed, setting back the receiver and pacing the kitchen floor. Finally, after a few moments of silence, Cory sat back in the chair and examined Beth's expression. "Did Clark ask about me after the game? Did he seem unhappy or upset because of our fight? Come on, Beth, tell me what happened. You're holding back on something."

"This is going to sound weird, but he acted like everything was fine. He's probably holding it all in like guys do," Beth quickly added as she reached over and touched Cory's arm. "You know how guys have to keep up that macho image."

"He didn't even ask if I was still there?" Cory said flatly, staring at the flecked yellow wallpaper.

"He didn't ask me," Beth said quietly, shrugging her shoulders.

"Where was he when you last saw him?" Cory questioned seriously.

"Ah, well, he was talking to Jon in the parking lot." Beth got up and started pacing nervously.

"And?" Cory said. "Come on, Beth, you're not telling me something, and you know I'm going to find out anyway, so I'd rather hear it from you."

"All right," Beth blurted. "He asked Jon if he could get some of the guys together tonight at Houlihans for a guys' night out."

"But we were supposed to go to the movies

tonight," Cory shouted as she jumped to her feet.

"I guess he figured you'd canceled out."

"Well, I haven't," Cory muttered, crossing back to the telephone to redial.

"I don't think you're going to find him home," Beth said quietly.

"And why not?" Cory asked with a questioning glance.

"Because he was giving Lisa a ride home from the game."

"Lisa!" Cory shouted, slamming down the receiver. "What is all this sudden attention to Lisa Pruitt? Shy, sweet, demure Lisa Pruitt!"

"I don't know, Cory, but it seems weird to me. The team thinks it's kind of bizarre, too."

"Oh, great, now the whole team is talking about me." Cory felt queasy again and plopped down in her chair ready to give up and cry. "What should I do?"

"I don't know, Cory," Beth said, comforting her. "Wait a minute, yes I do. We'll fight fire with fire."

"What do you mean?"

"If the guys are going to have a guys' night out, we'll have a girls' night out. We can all get together at my house and that'll show them that we can live without them."

Cory sighed. "Look, Beth, you don't have to cancel your date with Jon just because Clark and I are fighting."

"Who's canceling? Jon was so excited about going out with the guys he completely forgot about us. Let's call up the Puffs and invite them. We'll rent a movie and make some popcorn and fudge."

"Oh, I don't know, Beth. I don't think I could face the team tonight."

"You can do it, Cory. You're our leader. If you show them that Clark can't push you around, then maybe they'll stand up to their boyfriends, too."

"It does sound a lot better than sitting alone in my room. I have two requests, though."

"Name them," Beth said boldly.

"One, that we don't invite Lisa, and two, that *you* don't cook the fudge." The girls chuckled and started on their plans for the evening.

Chapter Ten

"Somebody change that record," Patti called. "I like Michael Jackson too, but that BAD album is starting to sound bad to me after the hundredth time."

"The rest of the Puffs are going to be sorry that they didn't cancel their plans for this event. I haven't had this much fun on a Friday night in a long time," Beth admitted as she stuffed another handful of popcorn in her mouth.

"Me neither," Vicki chimed in. "But I usually never do anything on Fridays anyway."

"Don't you go on a date to the movies once in a while?" Cory asked.

"Nah, nobody asks *me*."

"Why not?" Cory questioned more seriously. "You're one of the funniest people I know."

"Well, I may be funny, but I'm not pretty. You see, Cory, you may be athletic, but you also have a great little figure and big eyes and a cute smile. I'm close to six feet tall, have no waistline, and have the worst taste in clothes, not to mention that I've never worn makeup in my life," Vicki declared.

"I can't believe you've never been on a date," Cory answered with surprise. "Look, if it's makeup and clothes you're worried about, we can help you with a complete make-over, right, Beth?"

"Yeah, this could be a real challenge. No offense, Vicki!" Beth put in quickly as she evaluated Vicki's appearance.

"And when we finish with her, we can do Cory," Patti exclaimed.

"And then me," Beth added. "Before the evening's over, they'll think we're all Miss Americas."

"Or at least Elizabeth Ardens," Cory teased.

It had been an odd selection of girls at this party, Cory thought. She hadn't expected Vicki to be interested in a girls' night out, and although Patti wasn't one of her favorite people, she had figured she'd be on a hot date with some football player. No one mentioned the game that afternoon, or Clark. Cory figured that Beth had warned them, so after the first hour, Cory was able to forget about her breakup with Clark and enjoy the company of her female friends.

For the next two hours the Peterson home was turned into a beauty salon. The make-over workshop was in full swing, and since Beth had two older sisters there were plenty of supplies to work with. Patti was in charge of Cory's make-over. Cory would do Beth. Beth would do Patti, and the three of them would do Vicki. From hair to toenails, it was a complete process. And in the end they planned a final costume parade with fashions provided by "Peterson Sisters' Formal Wear."

"Your sisters are going to kill you, Beth, if they find out we've raided their closets to dress up," Cory warned.

"Then I suggest we don't tell them," Beth answered with a wink, picking out a sleek black cocktail dress with a bright red taffeta flounce. "Wait till you see the shoes that go with this. Anyway, Connie and Gayle are away for the weekend, so they'll never know." From down the hall the girls could hear Patti and Vicki giggling over their final wardrobe selections. "You'd better hurry up. The fashion show is in five minutes," Beth called.

Beth left the room, and Cory flipped through a few outfits, unsure of her choices. She lifted out a royal blue jumpsuit and a turquoise bridesmaid's dress. She stood in front of the full-length mirror that hung on the back of the door, considering her new image. For the first time in hours, her thoughts turned to Clark. Was he enjoying his evening out with the guys more than if they had gone to the movies? Cory was having a good enough time, but she couldn't imagine herself living every Friday night like this. Beth was trying hard to keep her from thinking of everything that had happened earlier, but now that she was alone again, all of the previous insecurities flooded back. "No," she said, cutting off the feeling of tears. She had made a firm resolution to keep it together, and she wasn't going to give up now. Besides, Patti would kill her if she ruined her make-over. Patti had washed her hair and then braided it into several strands. After her hair had dried they took out the braids and her hair was full and wavy, almost kinky. It looked soft and glamorous. Her makeup was much more dramatic than she usually wore it, with contour under her cheekbones and lip liner around her mouth. She stepped back and squinted her eyes, imagining herself older, more exotic. *It's what models look like*, she thought, *but is it right for me?* She held up the woolen jumpsuit, which was very tailored. Cory spun around once to get a better look. After one twirl, she stopped and smirked at her reflection. The old Cory would wear this. The preppy, self-controlled, run-the-show, tomboy Cory would have this jumpsuit in her closet, she thought. She hung it back up and inspected her second choice.

The gown was made of a medium-weight crepe material covered with chiffon. It had a sweetheart neckline and a small ruffle at the off-the-shoulder gather. The bodice was sleek-fitting and the skirt enormously full. It flowed for yards when she held out the edges of the dress. The chiffon was the same turquoise as the crepe, but with a floral pattern of blues and greens. "Well, Miss Scarlett, are you ready for the picnic with Ashley Wilkes?" Cory drawled, trying to muster an innocent grin. *This is a romantic, feminine dress, and perfect for your new image*, she thought, deciding on the gown. Quickly she tore off the sweatshirt she was wearing and slipped into the dress. It crinkled and rustled as she settled the sleeves low off her shoulders. She looked at her profile and wrapped the wide material belt around her waist, fumbling with a big bow in the back. She had to admit she liked what she saw, except for the rather flat bust line, so she ran into the bathroom looking for a few tissues to give her a more womanly look.

"Time's up, Cory," Beth called from the family room. "We're putting on the music and starting the show." Cory could hear the Frank Sinatra album start and giggled as she headed for the family room, stuffing some bathroom tissues in her bodice.

The Peterson basement had the perfect design for the girls' plans. They could make their entrances without being seen by each other. Beth paraded down the steps of the basement into the main room. Patti came from the guest bedroom off to the left. Vicki entered from behind the half-wall den area on the right, and Cory slid out of the bathroom at the opposite side of the room from Beth. They had promised not to laugh until they were all able to complete a full circle of the family room and then return to their starting places. Stifling snickers, the girls made it about five steps into the room before Beth broke out laughing and had to cover her face. Then it was a free-for-all.

"Look at you, you sexy thing!" Patti cried, twirling Beth around.

"I think you look smashing, Vicki," Cory said, complimenting her on her make-over. "You really look terrific."

"I don't think I'll ever get used to wearing the heels, but I might try investing in some makeup and hair spray. Do you think you can show up at my house before school every day to get me ready?" The group chuckled and Vicki made a turn, posed like a model.

"And don't you look like the Southern belle, Miss Cory," Beth said, smiling.

"That's Miss Corrine, to you." She pretended to fan herself as she curtsied and batted her eyes. "How kind of you lowly ladies in waiting to help me with my frock," Cory continued.

"What's this?" Patti proclaimed when she tugged on a loose piece of tissue sneaking out of Cory's bodice.

"Ah," Cory squealed as she crossed her arms over her chest. "That is my sacred beauty secret," she said, doubling over with laughter. Beth quickly uncovered another tissue and pulled out a long streamer. Before Cory could stop them, the girls were parading around her like a Maypole, draping her in pink toilet paper. They all laughed and hollered until they couldn't catch their breath.

"I wonder what Clark would say if he saw you like this," Patti said as she gasped for air. Suddenly, the room was dreadfully quiet, and all eyes were on Cory. Cory froze. Her stomach started churning, but she didn't have the hopeless sensation she'd felt earlier that day. She knew how hard everyone was trying to keep her mind off her problems, and a real sense of friendship and warmth embraced her. *What special friends,* Cory thought, *even Patti.*

"Clark who?" Cory said, blinking her eyes and shaking her head. The girls laughed feebly, not sure of Cory's reaction. "Actually," Cory said, twisting from under her paper banner, "I'd like to wrap him up in this stuff and flush it you know where."

"Whoa, watch out," Vicki said, covering her face.

"Cory's on the warpath," Patti added, hiding behind a large wing chair.

"I say we do it," Beth stated, standing firmly with her hands on her hips.

"Call me crazy, but somehow I don't think that Clark Williams is just going to stand around calmly as we shroud him in toilet paper," Cory said with a smirk.

"Not him, silly, his house. I say we buy a hundred rolls of TP and wrap his house and car. Just like on Mischief Night. Then after we finish his place, I say we do Jon's."

"I've got an old boyfriend I wouldn't mind adding to the list," Patti added, coming out from behind the chair.

"Vicki?" Beth quizzed, turning to their quarterback with a raised eyebrow.

"Well, there is this really cute guy in my English class," she admitted, blushing.

"Maybe we shouldn't do this. What if they

recognize us?" Cory said nervously. "I'm not going within fifty yards of Clark's house if he's at home."

"Just relax, Hughes," Patti said, sounding more like her old self. "We'll go in disguise."

"I'm all ready, then," Vicki said, posing. "There is no way anyone is going to recognize me in a green sequined top with a black satin skirt, black stockings, and heels."

"Let alone hair and makeup by Patti."

"And Cory."

"And Beth." The foursome laughed and inspected each other's "disguises."

"Okay, here's the plan," Patti started to explain.

"Who put you in charge?" Cory blurted out suddenly.

"Just hear me out. If you don't like the plan, you can put in your two cents' worth, all right?" Patti continued.

"Sorry, I didn't mean to sound so bossy." Patti and Cory looked at each other for a moment, evaluating their situation over the past few years. "I guess I've always been jealous because you're a cheerleader," Cory said finally.

"And I've always envied your popularity," Patti admitted. The girls smiled quietly at each other, and then Cory extended her hand.

"Truce?"

"Friends," Patti agreed, taking her hand.

"All right, enough of true confessions," Vicki interrupted. "I want to hear the plan, I don't care whose it is."

"Okay, I drove my folks' wagon over here and I think we should take that. We can all fit comfortably, plus it can hold all the toilet paper. We'll pool our finances and buy as much as we can."

"The cheap kind, you know the ones that come in a twelve-pack," Cory added.

"Right," Patti continued. "Then we figure out who lives where and go to work."

"Maybe we should figure that out before we go so we can plan our route."

"Great," Patti conceded.

"See, two heads work better than one," Beth said.

"Or criminal minds think alike," Vicki teased.

The girls got their coats and counted their money. Twenty-one dollars and sixty-two cents was going to buy a *lot* of bathroom tissue.

In the car, they buckled up and turned the radio on full blast to sing along with the Top 40 tune. Cory slouched down in the seat and gazed out at the stars. She was having second thoughts about their midnight escapade. Not that she thought there was anything criminal about what they were doing. But it was sad to know that she was having to resort to this behavior in order to be close to the guy she loved. She definitely was glad he wouldn't be at home.

"Okay. I say we get the cheapest brand and forget about the Cloud family," Vicki joked as they piled out of the car. The store manager must have thought that they were part of some kind of initiation for a sorority when they barged into the shop. Four teenage girls in formal attire were buying seven ten-packs of toilet paper. They were unable to maintain their dignity and burst out laughing uncontrollably several times until Cory took control and paid the clerk. She certainly felt weird, though, with her faded blue jeans peeking out from the bottom of her ball gown!

The plan was to do Vicki's crush's place first, Patti's old beau, and then finish up with Jon and Clark, since they only lived a few blocks from each other. They were surprised how fast they could toss twenty-seven rolls around. It didn't take long. After only two hours they rolled up to Clark's house with the headlights off.

"I'm so afraid of getting caught," Cory whispered to Beth.

"Now you know why I was so anxious to be done with Jon's," Beth answered back. They pulled up and hid the car behind the row of tall bushes. Carefully they divvied up the rolls and snuck out of the car. By now each girl had a specialty and went to work. Vicki's height made her the perfect choice for hard-to-reach tall tree branches. Beth was now famous for her intricate wrought-iron and light post work. Patti was a whiz with bushes and shrubs, and Cory nervously did artistic scalloped designs along the fences.

"I swear if this grass gets any wetter, you're going to have to dig me and these heels out of the ground," Vicki whispered.

"At least you're not having to stick the sides of your skirt in your jeans to keep it from dragging on the ground," Cory answered back.

"I think this is our best effort yet," Patti said, admiring their handiwork.

"Just a couple of final touches and we're through," Beth added. But before she had a chance to toss another roll, they heard a car coming down the street.

"Hide," Patti called, ducking around the side of the garage.

Other cars had passed by at the other guys' houses, but Cory knew in her gut that this wasn't just another car. It wasn't that she'd seen even a glimpse of the frame or a flash from the headlight; it *sounded* like Clark's car, and she panicked.

Vicki found a hiding place in the neighbor's bushes. Cory knew that Beth was nearby, but she couldn't see her from behind the garbage cans where she was hiding. Cautiously she looked around the backyard for a quick escape. She'd been here a million times before; why had she run to a place where the only way out was over a chain link fence ten feet high? The elementary school that bordered the Williamses' home would mean freedom, but it had to be used as a last-ditch effort. *Why did I get caught in the backyard with no escape?* she thought. *Why did Clark have to show up now? In five minutes we would have been gone.* Cory knew this hiding place wasn't going to shelter her if Clark started searching, and she knew he'd search.

They had left their unused rolls in various places on the lawn, a dead giveaway that they were still lurking about. Cory took a deep breath and closed her eyes tighter, trying to think. She heard a rustling noise by the back porch and saw Beth's shadow make a dash for a hedge that bordered the neighbor's driveway. Great, she thought sarcastically to herself. Patti was on the dark side of the garage with a straight shot for escape if Clark came around the right side of the house. Vicki was already in the neighbor's yard, and Beth had just cleared herself, too. Cory was the only criminal left, and she was crouched behind a metal can below the Great Wall of China.

"There's nobody in the front," Jon's voice called out. "They must be in the back someplace."

"Look at all this junk," Clark snarled as he gathered a fistful of Cory's handiwork. "I hope we catch them."

That was all that Cory had to hear to spring into action. Carefully she tucked the edges of the gown in her sash. She cowered behind the can until she could see that no one was coming. She stepped up on the metal lid of the fullest can and prayed that it wouldn't make a sound. With a toehold in the first link, she scaled the fence. First one leg over the top, and then the other. She was glad she'd left her jeans on or else her legs would have been scraped from top to bottom. As she turned her body around at the summit for the descent, her footing gave way. Before she had a chance to get a grip with her hands, her body slid downward. She prepared herself for the fall when she suddenly stopped dead, her feet dangling six inches off the ground. From what she could tell, the back of her dress had caught on the top of the jagged fence. It made a slight ripping sound when she tried to set her heels back into the fence, but there was no chance of freeing it. "Oh please, please let me get out of here," Cory mumbled to herself as she wriggled futilely.

"Well, well, well, what do we have here?" Clark said, pointing the beam of his flashlight on Cory's back. "I've caught a live one." Cory could hear the stomping of feet running in her direction. It must be the whole squad, she thought.

Before she knew it, Clark had scaled the fence and was staring at her as she dangled from the fence.

"Very attractive," he said, taking in the outfit. "Where's the rest of your little gang?"

"Just get me down from here, okay?" Cory suggested.

"And let you run away, before cleaning up this mess? I think not. Jon, see if you can unhook the dress, and I'll catch her from this side."

Cory wondered what he was feeling. He didn't sound angry, but he wasn't joking either. This was a very different sounding Clark, and something about him frightened her. But before she had a chance to further her evaluation, she was falling—right into Clark's arms.

Cory looked hopefully into Clark's face. But it was as blank and unemotional as if he'd just caught a sack of potatoes. So many nights Cory had dreamed of his embrace, and now she felt like a stranger. She rested her head on his shoulder and gave him a gentle squeeze, but he didn't respond. Instead he clutched her wrist and led her back around the playground of the school to the Williamses' front lawn. Neither of them said a word.

"So your friends abandoned you," he finally blurted when they came up the driveway. "I guess you'll have to clean this up by yourself. Any luck with the others, Jon?"

Jon came around from the backyard, but he wasn't alone. Standing next to him was Lisa! Timid, shy Lisa? She certainly wasn't losing any time putting her claws into Clark. What was she doing here? Cory thought as her blood began to boil. She stared daggers at her. Clark certainly hadn't wasted a second before finding a replacement for her!

"Nice dress, Cory," Jon teased. "And I've never seen you wear your hair like that before. You really look dolled up."

"Yeah, I thought you were only interested in football uniforms and strategies," Clark snapped. "You must have had a pretty hot date tonight."

"Obviously not as hot as yours," Cory shot back. "I thought this was guys' night out."

"Oh, you mean you're feeling left out since we didn't call you? That's right, you have to be in on everything, don't you?"

"This is ridiculous," Cory continued. "I'm sorry about what happened this afternoon. But I just don't see—"

"So am I," Clark interrupted flatly, "because it made me see you in a different light. Play football, coach the team, and manage its finances all at once. There's nothing the mighty Cory can't do!"

"That's not it at all," Cory interjected. "I don't see anything wrong with wanting to do your best. You do everything you want. I guess you just don't want any girl taking the spotlight away from you."

"Oh, you think you can do it better? Well, I'm here to tell you, you can't. If you were to put four guys against four girls, the guys would win hands down."

"You're just egotistical enough to believe that," Cory shouted back.

"You're on, baby," Clark snarled. "Anytime your four girls want a matchup against my four guys, you tell me."

"Clark, this is getting way out of hand. Just because I do something well doesn't take anything away from what you do. I don't know where you've gotten this crazy notion, but you're wrong," Cory pleaded.

"Then humor me." He was so angry that the veins on his neck began to bulge. "We'll have a contest Thursday to decide who's mightier. You arrange the events, since you like to run things, and the guys will show up." His voice was calm but angry.

"Fine," Cory said, throwing her arms up in

disgust. "It's not going to prove anything, but you seem to be set on a war. We'll show up at three; maybe you can wake up in time for *this* and make it there with your personal cheerleading squad by four." Cory glared at Lisa. Now she was really angry. What had been a week of misfortune and misunderstanding had turned into the battle of the sexes. Clark was acting like an ogre, and she didn't know why. She thought she still loved him, but she was sure having doubts.

The girls' station wagon suddenly pulled up, and Cory jumped in the open door. As the car pulled away from the curb, Cory could see Clark marching up the Williamses' front steps, followed meekly by Lisa.

That did it. "Oh, I get it now!" Cory shouted out the window. "You've added Lisa to your fan club because she's so meek she'll do anything you say. You can't take it when a girl has a mind of her own, can you?"

Chapter Eleven

"This whole thing is so stupid," Cory called to Beth the following Thursday as she completed marking the finish line for the "Battle of the Sexes" competition. "I can't believe we're really going through with it."

"Actually, I'm having a great time," Patti admitted while she set up the bright orange cones for the wheelbarrow race. "It's about time we had a chance to put those big lugs in their place."

"You don't like guys very much, do you?" Beth accidentally blurted. She quickly covered her mouth and prepared herself for the attack she was sure would follow. Patti stood stunned for a moment and then glanced at Beth, Cory, and Vicki, who waited for her reaction.

"I guess I'm still feeling burned," she said softly, shrugging her shoulders. "I went with this guy all last spring and summer, and he dropped me the first week of school for some sophomore. I was really nuts about him, too."

She sat down on the grass and tried to hide the emotion in her voice. "I didn't realize I was sounding so antimale these days, but I guess I don't fool you guys."

"You shouldn't have to suffer all by yourself," Cory said, sitting next to her and putting her arm around her shoulder. "Breakups are the hardest things to deal with. I've shed an ocean of tears this last week. If it weren't for the three of you, I'd be a basket case."

"You were a basket case before," Vicki teased. "Now you just have an excuse." She sat next to Patti, and Beth came over and filled in the circle by taking the spot by Cory.

"All for one and one for all," Beth said, giving Cory's hand a squeeze. The other girls joined in, and they sat quietly for a moment. "Thanks, you guys, I feel a lot better," Cory said.

"Me too," Patti added.

"That's what friends are for," Beth said, smiling.

"Well, you won't be completely cured until you have Clark back," Beth reassured, "but we'll be around until you do." The best friends hugged and then went off to take care of the final preparations for the meet.

"I still think this is a dumb idea—I still love Clark," Cory said, taking a big green duffel bag from the wagon that held their supplies. "But he made me so mad the other night."

"Have you had a chance to be alone together since then?" Vicki asked.

"Not really. Every time I've tried to approach

him in the halls, Lisa is right beside him. I'm not sure what's going on with those two, but I can tell you this, I don't like it one bit." Cory tugged at the drawstring at the top of the bag and finally pushed it over in disgust.

"Take it easy," Beth said, taking her turn at undoing the knot. "Jon told me that they're just friends."

"I seriously doubt if Lisa thinks of it that way," Cory said. "Who would have ever guessed that shy, meek little Lisa could be such a vixen underneath?"

"They always say to watch out for the silent types."

"It's just that she's everything I'm not. She's tall and slender with blond hair and blue eyes. A quiet follower who isn't going to take sides or speak up unless spoken to. And if that's what Clark is looking for, there's nothing I can do about it."

"If that's all he wants, then you're better off without him. But somehow I don't see Clark being attracted to those qualities," Beth said, finally getting the knot untied. The girls dumped the contents onto the practice field and began sorting the equipment. "He likes you because you're athletic and strong. Just because you like sports doesn't mean you're not feminine."

"I hope he feels that way," Cory sighed.

"We'll find out after today's challenge," Patti added.

"I just hope I'm not making the biggest mistake of my life," Cory said with a shrug.

"Well, it's too late to back out now. Half the school is talking about the Battle of Sexes. I heard that kids were even taking bets on who wins," Vicki announced.

"I can't believe that Clark and I having a fight has become the latest school event." Cory covered her face with her hands and shook her head. "I hate this already."

"I suggest you put on your happy face, because here comes the first group of spectators," Patti said, adjusting her jersey. The girls had decided to wear their uniforms since they were the easiest things to move around in.

Cory and Beth turned around to see about two dozen peers headed for the field where the event was to take place.

"We should have sold tickets," Vicki said with a grin. "Maybe then we could've paid off these outfits."

"I heard that the girls' field hockey team had their practice early so they could come and cheer us on," Beth added.

"Yes, and our team has made up a banner to hang on the bleachers," Patti said. "I can't wait to see the looks on their faces when they see the events we've cooked up." The four girls giggled and hurried to set up the equipment needed for the four events they had designed.

Clark had only insisted that the contest consist of things that would test their strength, balance, speed, and stamina. He hadn't made any suggestions, so the girls had put on their

114

thinking caps to come up with a competition that would be fair, but fun. The test of strength would be an old-fashioned human wheelbarrow race. Two of the team members would be involved. One would stand upright and hold the ankles of the other teammate, while she used the strength of her arms to maneuver around the orange cones set up on the field. When they finished the zigzag, they would switch positions—only this time the person on the bottom would be upright—and they would rush back on a straight course to where they had started.

The second test would be for balance. Again two teammates would go for each side. An egg would be placed on the top of each contestants foot. Then the contestants would follow a path to the opposite end of the field, trying to keep the egg from falling off.

The test for speed was Cory's best event. It was a running race like any other, only the competitors wore swim fins.

For the final event, everyone would participate. It was an obstacle course of sorts. Competitors would carry beach balls between their legs, play hopscotch, jump on pogo sticks, throw Frisbees through a hoop, and finally crawl a tunnel to ring a bell with their teeth, signifying the finish.

Each contest would have specific points given for first through fourth place, with first receiving fifteen points and fourth receiving two. The team with the most points at the end of the match was the winner.

The events were all set up by two-thirty, and quite a crowd had gathered to cheer the teams on. *It's too bad we can't get this kind of support for our weekly games,* Cory thought. *But maybe this can be the start of something big.* She started to feel pregame nerves in her stomach and decided to warm up on the grass. In the middle of her stretching routine she felt a tap on her shoulder. *Clark!* She looked up to see Bryan Thomas smiling down at her.

"Good luck today," he said, taking her hand to help her up off the ground. "If you're as good at this as you are at making pancakes, you're sure to win."

"Thanks, Bryan," Cory said, a little flustered. "It's nice to know we have some male support on our side."

"Well, I always thought that the school should be more active in women's sports."

"Not just sports," Cory stated. "But politics, scholarships, honors clubs. I'll bet you didn't realize that there are two clubs in this school that don't allow girls." Cory placed her hands on her hips and glared at Bryan.

"So that's what this is all about," he said mildly. "I'll listen to any of your complaints."

"I'm sorry," Cory apologized, smiling. "I shouldn't take it out on you."

"How about if you explain it to me over dinner after the race? You look like you could use a friend."

Cory shyly lowered her head and kicked at the grass. She liked Bryan—he was hand-

116

some, kind, and intelligent. But she wasn't ready to give up on Clark. She wanted to hold onto the idea that after the contest everything would go back to normal. He would sweep her off her feet, apologize for being such a jerk, and then the two of them would celebrate. "I don't know, Bryan," Cory answered hesitantly. "I'm not sure if I'd be very good company."

"It's okay, you don't have to give me your answer right now. I'll check with you after the match." Bryan flung his jacket over his shoulder and headed for the bleachers. Before he climbed up the steps he turned and gave Cory the thumbs-up sign.

"Come on, Cory," Patti called. "Here comes the opposing team."

Clark was coming up the hill with an entourage of football players. He looked confident and happy. Cory's heartbeat quickened, and she thought about running over to him, throwing her arms around his neck, and kissing him until all of their problems melted away. She wanted to call this whole fiasco off. She closed her eyes and started to move in his direction, but when she opened them, all she could see was Lisa slipping her arm into the crook of his arm and giving it a squeeze. Cory stopped short. Her competitive spirit rekindled as she felt pangs of jealousy. *How dare she hang all over him*, she thought. *And how dare he let her do it.*

"Forget it, she doesn't mean anything to him," Beth said knowingly as she approached her friend.

"Let the games begin," Coach Lang, one of the referees for the event, called. The crowds cheered, and Cory glanced at Clark with mixed feelings.

"What's all this junk for?" Jon quizzed as he looked at the cones, flippers, and eggs.

"That's part of the equipment for the races," Beth said, sauntering toward her boyfriend.

"In what kind of race do you use swim fins?" Clark snickered, holding up the black flipper.

"We asked you if you wanted an explanation of the races on Monday," Cory said, "but you said there wasn't anything we could come up with that you couldn't do on the spot." The couple stared at each other while Miss Flory, the other referee, explained each round.

"Each team member has to compete in two events, one of those being the final obstacle course," Miss Flory continued. "So as soon as the fellas have decided who is running which event we'll get started."

Since the first race was the wheelbarrow and a test of strength, the girls chose Vicki and Patti, and the guys picked Bob and Dan.

"You can do it," Beth and Cory cheered to their teammates as Vicki clutched Patti's ankles at the starting line.

"This is sissy kids' stuff," Clark said, slapping Bob on the back.

"Remember, whoever finishes through the cones first gets fifteen points, and whoever crosses the finish line first gets an additional five. So—on your mark, get set, GO!" Miss Flory called.

Both teams got off to a shaky start.

"Keep going," Cory yelled through cupped hands.

"Just like in practice," Beth continued as she ran along the sidelines.

The crowds obviously had chosen sides, and the shrill sounds of the girls cheering outweighed the male supporters. The race was going neck and neck until the fourth cone, where Patti's hand slipped into a rut and her elbow collapsed. It gave the guys a chance to get ahead at the final cone.

"That's okay," Cory screamed. "You can catch them on the return. We're behind you all the way."

The crowds continued the chant, filling the fall air with sounds of enthusiasm.

"The cheers seem to be working," Beth called to Cory.

"Yeah, look at those girls go," Cory answered. With Patti at the helm, Vicki was only feet away from reaching the finish line. Bob's arms were too bulky to let him get an even rhythm. The guys lumbered across the finish line far behind the girls. The crowd went crazy, and each side felt as if it had won.

"The guys took first and fourth, receiving seventeen points," Coach Lang announced. "And the girls are right on their heels with the second and third place totals of fifteen points."

"All right, Beth, show them what you're made of," Patti cried as Beth ambled toward the starting line for her event.

"Is this a cooking event?" Jon teased, looking down at the eggs near his feet.

"Ooh, ooh, ooh," Clark said in his best French chef accent. "We vill see who can make ze soufflé ze quickest today." The guys laughed, proud of their previous victory.

"You're just a barrel of laughs," Cory muttered, glaring at Clark.

"Okay, quiet down," Miss Flory said, explaining the event. "The goal of this event is to cross the finish line without scrambling an egg under your foot. If the egg falls off the top of your foot, you must go back to the starting line and begin again. Any questions before we start?"

"Hey, Jon, this should be a piece of cake. You have the largest feet in the whole school," Clark added, elbowing Jon in the ribs. "We'll have to worry about your walking, though." Once again the boys chuckled with confidence.

"We'll see who laughs last," Patti called before giving Beth the okay sign.

"Just take your time, Beth," Cory instructed. "Try to forget that Jon is your boyfriend. I'm really sorry about getting you into this mess."

"When are you going to learn that this isn't your problem? It's a bigger picture than Cory versus Clark. It has to do with pride, school support, and chauvinism. Now I have a chance to prove my stuff, too." Beth smiled at her buddy.

"Ready, set, GO!" Miss Flory shouted, starting the race.

It was like a page out of the tortoise and

the hare. Jon bolted ahead but only went a few feet before crushing the egg under his sneaker. Beth slowly inched her way down the field, carefully balancing her egg. The crowds cheered and screamed, and it didn't take long before Jon was only inches away from Beth.

Then it happened again. Jon's egg toppled off the laces and squashed under his foot. The male team members groaned and Jon ran back to the starting line. Beth kept her concentration and moments later crossed the finish line to the whoops and hollers of the female supporters.

"The score now stands: men 27, women 30," Miss Flory announced with a certain amount of pride. Once again the fans started chanting their support for the girls.

"Let's keep this moving," Coach Lang proclaimed as he started setting up the cones for the next competition.

Cory nervously approached the start and picked up a pair of swim fins. She noticed that Clark was walking toward her. She hoped he was coming over to wish her luck but soon found out that they were going to be pitted against each other in the contest.

"I guess it's you and me on this one," Clark quietly said, staring at the pile of flippers. "Are we really going to have to jump over those cones in this scuba gear?"

Cory felt silly, and again the whole contest seemed ridiculous. She wished she could hit a time machine button and forget everything that had happened in the past few weeks. "I'm sorry," Cory mumbled to herself.

"What's that?" Clark asked, looking to Cory like a lost puppy dog.

"Okay, Williams, it's all up to you," Jon said, making his usual interruption.

"I'll do my best," Clark answered, still gazing at Cory. He picked up several fins, trying to push them over his shoes.

"I thought I knew your shoe size, but I guess I was wrong about that, too," Cory said, picking out another flipper. "Are any of them close?"

"I think I can wear these with my socks." He sighed, tugging off his sneakers and squeezing into the large black fins.

"Remember that this contest is not only a test of speed," Coach Lang began, "but ten seconds will be added to the score if any cones are knocked over. Are both teams ready?"

"Ready," Cory and Clark answered together.

"Then let the best man win," the coach said. "Sorry, Cory," he added with a smile. "May the best 'contestant' win."

Clark and Cory started out even. Clark's long legs sailed over the cones easily. Cory had practiced diligently all week and had finally mastered the art of getting her short legs over the hurdles. She knew that whether she won or lost, she'd do her best.

They were still head to head when they reached the second to the last cone and out of the corner of her eye Cory saw Clark stumble. The tip of one fin caught the cone, and he went sprawling facedown in the wet grass. Without thinking, Cory stopped and turned toward her boyfriend. His face was spattered with mud and grass stains, and his expression was one of embarrassment and defeat.

"What are you doing?" Patti shouted. "Keep going." She motioned toward the finish, but Cory couldn't move. She wanted to say something to Clark, but her voice wouldn't work either.

"Do it for the team!" Vicki screamed. "He's okay."

Before Cory could decide what to do, Clark was back on his feet and racing toward the finish line. Cory's muscles didn't respond at first, and Clark raced past her. Her concern turned to anger, and she leapt into action, quickly making up lost ground. Her face was tightly drawn, and her fists were clenched as her arms stretched toward the finish line. She stuck out her chin as a final effort and crossed the chalk at the same time as Clark. Both teams rushed to the two, cheering wildly. Clark was swept over to the men's bench.

"You gave us quite a scare," Patti said, congratulating her.

"We thought you might give up," Vicki added.

"Never," Cory answered, realizing that Clark had only thought of the match.

"Because of the tipped cone, and the ten-second penalty, the women have increased their lead to 45. But the men are still in there with 37 points," Coach Lang called through his bullhorn over the applauding group.

"We'll take a fifteen-minute break to set up for the final event," Miss Flory said, taking the megaphone from Coach Lang. Cory gulped some water and dabbed her forehead with a towel from her tote bag. Then she flung the towel over her shoulder and walked with determination toward the men's bench and Clark.

"Are you all right?" she asked from behind. The other guys glanced at her and then moved away to prepare for the final competition.

"Sure," he answered, turning to face her. His eyes no longer looked cold and angry as they had the week before, but they didn't have their usual sparkle either.

"No bruises?" Cory persisted.

"Just my pride," he said, trying to smile. "You looked really good out there."

"I had a terrific coach," Cory eagerly added, returning his smile.

"Come on, Cory," Beth called, running over to join them. "We need to review our tactics for the obstacle course. Hi, Clark, hope you're okay."

"Just great," Clark said, lowering his head and slapping his jeans.

"I hate this," Cory said through clenched teeth as they walked back to their bench. "How are we ever going to get back together this way?"

"I don't know," Beth said, putting an arm around her shoulder. "All I know is that we've gone this far and it's too late to turn back now."

"I guess you're right," Cory said with a sigh. "But I still hate this."

The girls walked the rest of the way back to the bench in silence, listening to the students encouraging the girls' team.

"No wonder guys go out for sports," Vicki said, staring up into the bleachers.

"What makes you say that?" Beth questioned.

"It's all an ego trip," Patti continued. "Who wouldn't want a stadium full of fans. Just listen to them." For a moment the girls stared up into the cheering group. It was a strange but invigorating sensation.

"It's too bad the whole Puff team doesn't get to experience this rush," Cory said flatly.

"Oh, yes, isn't this exciting?" Lisa's voice broke their trance. The others frowned at Lisa but she continued to smile at them. Then they drifted away, leaving Cory alone with Lisa. "You all are doing so well."

"I thought you'd be cheering for the guys' team," Cory said, picking up the water bottle again.

"Oh, I'm rooting for everyone, really." She shifted her weight and started to twist her index finger around a gold chain that encircled her neck. On the bottom of the chain was Clark's ring!

"Is that Clark's ring?" Cory practically shouted, lunging toward Lisa.

"Why, yes, it is," Lisa answered, beaming.

"Where did you get it?" Cory demanded.

"I don't think that's any of your business," Lisa said, taking a step back.

"I don't believe Clark gave you his ring."

"You can believe anything you like, but I am wearing his ring."

"On *my* necklace," Cory said, reaching for the chain. Lisa tugged away, protecting her treasure.

"You're just jealous because Clark wants me instead of you. Well, maybe if you acted more like a girl, you wouldn't have lost him. But now that he's mine, I'll never let him go."

"We'll see about that," Cory said, enunciating every syllable. She turned her back on Lisa and marched toward her teammates. She was so angry and hurt—and confused; she didn't know who to blame, Clark or Lisa. She still loved him so much, but she couldn't believe that he had forgotten her so easily. Cory looked in Clark's direction to see Lisa give him a kiss on the cheek.

"Are you all right?" Beth asked. "Do you think you can run the race?"

"Not only will I run it," Cory declared, "I'll WIN it."

Chapter Twelve

"I'm really glad you changed your mind about going out after the race," Bryan said, handing Cory a soda. "I thought you'd be tired, but the way you conquered that obstacle course was awesome."

"Thanks," Cory said, trying to muster up a smile and some enthusiasm.

"Really," Bryan added, his brown eyes glowing. "They're going to be talking about this contest until graduation."

"Oh, I hope not," Cory answered as her mind flooded with a thousand pictures. She had been surprised at herself in the final event, too. Her feelings of despair and confusion had changed to jealousy and anger. With every obstacle she'd had to face, she became more determined and stronger. When it came down to the final evaluation, she had come out with the best time and the least number of penalties. The girls had won first, third, and fourth, adding another twenty-two points to their first-place victory. Unfortunately, Cory didn't feel that great about winning. Losing Clark made her feel like she'd come in last place. The cheers of the crowd hadn't affected her as much as the sight of Lisa comforting Clark at the end of the match. When Bryan had come up to her and given her a congratulatory hug, she'd clung on, trying to squeeze the pain away. She had still been staring at Clark when she'd agreed to go out with Bryan.

"So, where would you like to get a bite to eat?" Bryan said, breaking Cory's daydream.

"I don't care," Cory answered. "You decide." She slipped on her jean jacket and then held her purse and notebook close to her chest. Cory liked Bryan a lot as a friend, but she wanted to have her arms full in case he tried to hold her hand.

They walked silently through the school parking lot, interrupted only by well-wishers congratulating Cory on her performance. Cory concentrated on the sounds of gravel and crunching leaves under her feet. She couldn't keep her mind off Clark and the sorrowful look on his face when Coach Lang had announced that the girls had won. Vicki and Patti had jumped up so high that it looked as if they had springs in their feet. Beth's reaction was similar to Cory's. She was glad and proud of her accomplishment, but the thrill wasn't complete knowing that she'd had to defeat Jon to do it.

Jon had been great about the whole affair, though. He had waited outside the girls' locker room for Beth, and they were going to spend a quiet evening together watching TV. Cory had felt a twinge of jealousy but was glad that this whole fiasco hadn't hurt their relationship the way it had hers.

"Are you in the mood for anything special?" Bryan said, trying to get the conversation rolling.

"I think I'm too keyed up now to think straight," Cory lied.

Bryan opened the passenger side of his royal blue Mustang, and Cory slid into the car, relieved that it had bucket seats.

"Well, how about some Chinese, then? We can even get some take-out at Fong's and bring it to the park."

"No, not Fong's," Cory blurted. Bryan looked at her, stunned by her violent reaction. "I got sick on it once and haven't gotten over it yet." She'd lied again, but she couldn't believe that of all the places to suggest, Bryan had chosen the spot where she and Clark liked to go. Many summer nights after the pool had closed they had gone and ordered egg rolls and a Fong's special. It was their spot, and she vowed then and there never to go back unless Clark was with her.

"All right, then how about burgers? We can go to the drive-through and still get to the bike races on time."

"B-bike races?" Cory stammered.

"Yeah, I know you like to watch them. Tonight's the last show for the season, a special farewell to summer."

A farewell to a lot of things, Cory thought.

Why did he have to pick the bike races, too? she wondered. Thursday night had always meant Chinese food and the bike races with Clark. Since many of the great bicyclists trained at Northbrook, it was always an exciting evening of cheap entertainment.

Bryan babbled on about some cyclist that he'd been following all summer, and before she knew it they were ordering burgers and fries and heading back to the track.

"Do you want to eat these in the car or take them up in the bleachers?" Bryan asked.

"We might as well go in. Besides, we'll probably get better seats."

Actually, Cory was a little afraid to stay alone in the car with Bryan; she didn't feel much like conversation, and if they got into the stadium, there were bound to be other kids there for Bryan to talk to. Maybe they could even sit with a group.

Bryan opened her door, and they wandered through the half-full parking lot to the entrance. Northbrook was actually known as the speed-skating capital of the country. Famous Olympic skaters like Sheila Young Anchowicz trained here in the winter and then did bicycling to keep in shape during the summer months. It was a large outdoor stadium with a warming house and snack bar. The center of the track was still filled with green grass, which would be covered with ice in only a few short months. The track itself was asphalt and sloped gradually toward the stands. The cyclists and their families, trainers, and coaches set up various equipment and tools on the grassy part, leaving the spectators to picnic in the stands.

Cory and Bryan found a place fairly close to the start/finish line, even though the competition had already begun.

"Isn't this great?" Bryan sighed, filling his lungs with the crisp fall air.

"It's my favorite time of year," Cory confessed as she started to relax. "Which cyclists have you been following?"

"George Garner's son—I think he has a lot of potential," Bryan said, pointing to a lanky boy with well-defined calf muscles. "They sure are dedicated. I don't know if I could keep up with all the training."

"You're just chicken to shave your legs," Cory teased, reacting like her old self. Because of the many falls the racers endured, it became easier and healthier for them to keep their legs smooth.

For the next forty minutes Cory enjoyed herself. The burger had revived her a bit, and she and Bryan were betting on winners by the colors of their jerseys.

"I think that any guy wearing hot pink has got to be a winner," Cory declared, betting a French fry on the outcome of the next time trial.

"You're on," Bryan challenged, placing a fry on the paper next to Cory's. "My potatoes are on the man in gold."

The race was a long one, and both riders were skilled. But in the final lap the "man in gold" had been triumphant. Cory laughed as Bryan proudly gobbled the prize.

"It's good to see you laugh again," Bryan said.

"I'm sorry," Cory answered shyly. "It's just that it's been a tough few weeks, and I haven't had a lot to laugh about."

"Well, I want you to know that I'm here if you need me. Even if it's only a shoulder to cry on. If you haven't guessed by now, I think you're kind of special." His brown eyes softened as he took Cory's hand and gently gave it a squeeze. He had such a warm touch, Cory thought. He delicately set her hand back in her lap and continued to watch the race in progress.

Cory watched him and thought about the things he'd done for her in the past. Beth had been right; he did like her. Bryan was handsome in an intellectual-looking way, Cory thought as she watched the breeze play with his straight, dark brown hair. He had a long straight nose, a profile of strength and authority. His frame was long and lanky. He had a square jaw and a full mouth that revealed beautiful, straight teeth when he smiled. It's a nice face, Cory decided.

"You want to bet on the next race?" Bryan asked as he turned to face Cory, who was still staring at him.

"We've run out of fries," Cory said, shaking the little bag upside down.

"Well, there must be something else that we could wager." There was a gleam in Bryan's

eyes that Cory knew well. She and Clark often bet on the races, but they usually bet
kisses—that way no one ever lost. Was Bryan
suggesting the same wager?

"I do smell hot apple cider coming from the
concession stand," Cory suggested casually.
"This air is getting a little chilly and I could
use some, no matter what. Winner pays?"

"Okay," Bryan answered, somewhat disappointed. "I'll put my apples on Garner; he's in
this next time trial, and this is his best event."

"Then I'll stick with the guy in the hot pink
jersey. He wouldn't let me down."

The race was another exciting one. The
experts paced themselves and strategically ma-
neuvered to the inside position. Two competitors bumped wheels and sent one of the
racers sprawling on the grass. The other re-
cuperated and rushed ahead to join the pack.

"You forget that they're going about sixty
miles an hour," Bryan said, shaking his head.

"I hope he's all right," Cory whispered, still
watching her man.

The last lap started, and the pace quickened as the remaining five shot around another curve. The contest was really between
three riders, Cory's and Bryan's choices and
a mysterious man in black. Each rider flat-
tened out lower, practically resting on the
handlebars. These bikes were specially designed with no brakes or gears. The racers
were held on to the pedals with toe clips, and
their success depended on who could push
himself the most. The fans started to cheer,

and Cory found herself standing to root for her man in pink. The whir of rubber tires sliding over asphalt heightened as the trio passed Cory and Bryan. Only moments later the man in black hurled forward, leaving the other two to fight over second and third.

"Well, I'm glad I didn't bet a hundred dollars on that one," Bryan said, sitting back down.

"It looks like my man in pink came in third, so I'll still buy the cider. I need to call my mom and tell her I'm here anyway," Cory said as she reached down to pick up her purse.

"Do you need any help carrying the cups?"

"Thanks, I'll manage. Besides, here comes one of your friends from the student council. I'll be back in a minute." Cory was glad she was beginning to relax. She decided being out with Bryan was more like going out with a friend than a date. Somehow that way she didn't have to feel guilty or disloyal.

As she stepped down the bleachers, she saw that the stands were full of students from Glenbrook. She stopped and chatted with some girls from the Puff team who congratulated her on her win in the Battle of the Sexes.

The warming house was crowded with other hungry and thirsty spectators. No one was at the phone, so Cory made her phone call first. The cider would stay hotter that way. She reached into her jeans pocket and pulled out a quarter and a small slip of paper. What could this be? she wondered, unfolding the scrap. The paper was worn on the creases, so

Cory knew it had been in her pocket for a while. It might have even gone through the washing machine a time or two. No matter how many times her mother told her, she always forgot to empty her pockets before putting her clothes in the laundry.

Carefully she unfolded the note. The ink had faded, but she recognized Clark's handwriting immediately.

Good luck against Wilmette in the football game today. You're the greatest!!!
                                    Yours, Clark.

Her stomach dropped, and she felt her heart pound against her chest. That had only been a month ago! Cory felt weak as she held the note tightly in her fist. She called home to tell her mom that she'd be home a little later. She knew she sounded shaky but didn't want to explain. As Cory turned around to hang up the receiver, she noticed Lisa out of the corner of her eye.

Lisa was standing outside the girls' rest room chatting with a group of girls Cory didn't know. Cory stared at her as she laughed and giggled, oblivious to Cory's presence. But when she started flaunting Clark's ring dangling from her necklace, Cory wanted to cry. She huddled tighter in the telephone shell to compose herself. Maybe the reason Clark had never said he loved her was that he never had. They had shared so much together, it was hard to believe. But Lisa now had the ring she'd worn only a week ago, and that had to mean something.

Suddenly a wave of nausea swept through Cory as the truth of the relationship started to piece itself together like a jigsaw puzzle. She had only been a summer romance, jilted the same way Patti had been. She wanted to rip that ring from Lisa's neck, but she stayed hidden. She vowed not to become bitter like Patti, but she knew she wasn't ready for anything new with Bryan, either. She wouldn't forget about Clark for a long, long time. Cory sighed and walked bravely past Lisa and her friends to stand in line for the cider.

"You were really good today," Clark's familiar voice said gently from behind.

Cory wanted desperately to whirl around and hug him, but instead she answered calmly, "Thanks, but to tell you the truth, I didn't enjoy it very much."

"Me neither," Clark answered. They still hadn't looked at each other. "The other girls on your team seemed to be pretty excited."

"Oh, Patti and Vicki were, but I think Beth was worried about hurting Jon's feelings."

"That's nice."

"Yeah, it sure is," Cory sighed. "I really never intended for our differences to cause a school uprising."

"I didn't, either," Clark said, moving closer so that Cory could feel his breath on her neck. For a few moments neither one said a word. Cory was too busy trying to keep from falling apart. At one point she wasn't even sure if Clark was still standing behind her. She wanted to turn around and look but knew that she wouldn't be able to face him if he was.

"I saw you and Bryan Thomas sitting together," Clark said, finally breaking the silence.

Cory was the next in line and ordered the two ciders. She picked them up and for the first time looked at Clark as she started back to the stands. "And *you're* here with Lisa."

"I'm sorry," Clark mumbled. He looked tired and lost as his gray eyes met Cory's.

"Me, too," Cory answered, the lump in her throat making it difficult to swallow. She lowered her head and numbly walked back to the stands.

For the rest of the match, Cory was practically silent. She felt bad because she knew that Bryan was trying desperately to get her to enjoy herself. It had worked earlier, but seeing Clark and Lisa had opened the wound again. Bryan was a wonderful friend, but that was it. No matter how kind he was, he wasn't Mr. Right. Clark was, and if she and Clark weren't going to be together, she was going to need time, a lot of time, to get over him.

"The final competition this evening will be the popular Miss'in Outs," the commentator announced.

"Do you mind taking me home?" Cory interrupted. This had been hers and Clark's favorite event, and she knew she wouldn't be able to sit through it without breaking down.

Chapter Thirteen

"You were inspiring yesterday," a sophomore girl called to Cory when she approached her locker the following morning. There were congratulatory notes taped to the metal door and even a big pink and purple bow. A long banner attached to the ribbon read, "Go Puffs, beat Deerfield." In small print at the bottom it said, "Good Luck Cory," and was signed "The Puff cheerleading squad."

"We don't have a cheerleading squad," Cory mumbled to herself as she turned the combination lock.

"I think we're a hit," Beth said cheerfully, meeting Cory at the locker. "There are banners and good-luck signs all over the school."

"To tell the truth," Cory admitted, "with all the planning for yesterday's event, I completely forgot about today's game."

"I know, we missed two practices this week."

"Do you think they'll let us play?" Cory asked, getting her English and science texts from the top shelf.

"Are you kidding!" Beth answered, laughing. "After yesterday, I think they'd give us the key to the city."

"All this attention is pretty amazing," Cory admitted as she shut the locker door. "Does your locker look like this, too?"

"Just about. All the girls on the squad got the bows and the banner. Who do you think our cheerleaders could be?"

"I haven't got the foggiest notion. Maybe some of the freshman girls who supported us yesterday."

"I saw you at the bike races with Bryan," Beth confided as they headed to their first class. "But when I looked for you after the final match, you two were gone. Anything you'd like to tell me?" Beth's voice was light and inquisitive.

"Yeah, I'm still in love with Clark. Bryan's just a friend, and I asked him to take me home before the end."

"Sorry," Beth apologized. "I just thought you might have found a way to mend a broken heart."

"Did you know that Clark gave his ring to Lisa?" Cory blurted as they reached the science lab.

"Jon said he saw it, too, but I thought it was crazy. I can't believe Clark would do such a thing. You must be sick about it. What a mistake Clark is making."

"The mistake's all mine," Cory said half to herself. "If I hadn't been so set on proving my equality, maybe we'd still be together."

"You don't mean that," Beth scolded as the girls sat at their desks. "If Clark really loved you, it wouldn't matter if you were the captain of the guys' wrestling team."

"You're right," Cory sighed. "That's just the problem. He doesn't love me. You were in the Battle of the Sexes, too, but Jon didn't break up with you."

"It's my peanut butter cookies," Beth said, trying to lighten the conversation. "He can't live without my peanut butter cookies."

The first hour bell rang, and class started. Cory tried to concentrate on chemistry, but her mind wandered to Clark. By the end of the hour she had made a decision. She wanted to talk to him face-to-face. She couldn't imagine the thought of avoiding him for the rest of the year. She wanted to try to convince him one last time that they were good together. If he wanted to stay with Lisa, then at least he would know that she still cared. She knew the others would think she was a fool for trying, but she had to be honest about her feelings. If Clark rejected her, at least she'd know she'd tried and could go on without him. As her grandmother often said, "You can't hold on to something you never had."

All day Cory searched for Clark. She waited outside his classroom doors, stood at his locker during his lunch hour, and even called his house to see if he was sick. But he didn't seem to be anywhere. Cory was obsessed with the need to talk to him, and she knew she wouldn't rest until she did. If she could only catch him before the football match, they could have their talk, and then neither of them would have to feel awkward in front of the rest of the team. With new hope, she waited in the gym, pacing in front of the boys' locker room.

"Hey, Cory," Vicki called from the top of the stairs. "Did you hear the news?"

"What news?" Cory asked, still keeping her eyes on the locker doors. Vicki glanced at Patti, who had come in with her. "What's with you two, what's the big news?"

"You're the one who wanted to tell her," Patti said, nudging Vicki's elbow.

"Well, somebody tell me!" Cory demanded, setting her hands on her hips.

"We thought it might be easier hearing it from one of us," Vicki muttered.

"Hearing what?"

"That Clark resigned as coach of the Puff team," Patti finally blurted.

Cory stood stunned for a moment. She couldn't believe he would quit. The whole idea of a girls' team had been his. He couldn't just quit because of everything that had happened between them. He had committed himself to the Puffs; the team needed his guidance. "I've got to talk to him," Cory said as she picked up her coat and purse to head for the door.

"He's not in school," Vicki yelled. "He hasn't been all day."

"Neither has Lisa," Patti added. "I'm sorry, Cory. I hate to be the bearer of bad news, but we thought you'd rather hear it from a friend."

Cory slowly turned around to face her buddies. The looks on their faces were almost as pained as the way she felt. They really did care about her, and right now that felt like the most important thing in the world. Suddenly all the strength and confidence she'd been showing lately drained out of her and she couldn't hold the tears back any longer. Beth rushed into the gym just as the others were leading Cory into the girls' locker room.

"I guess you heard the news," Beth said, handing a tissue to Cory, who was sitting on the bench. "The janitor said he saw him here an hour before school started. He was with some of the other football team guys. But they left way before the first bus arrived."

"It's all my fault," Cory wailed. "He never should have resigned as the coach."

"It's not your fault," Beth soothed. "If he resigned, he must have done it because he didn't think that he was doing enough for the team."

Cory took a deep breath and sighed. She looked at each one of her friends and gave them a hug. "You guys have sure had to put up with a lot from me lately. Thanks for hanging in there."

"Remember, that's what friends are for," Beth said, returning the squeeze.

"Well, I guess the best thing I can do now is go out there and play a fantastic game," Cory said, wiping her eyes for the twentieth time.

"That's the Cory we know!" Vicki encouraged.

"At least you won't have to deal with Lisa

today," Patti chimed in. "If you're not in school the day of the game, you're ineligible to play."

"She's right," Beth said, smiling.

"Well, thank goodness for small favors," Cory said, relaxing a bit.

Moments later the rest of the team started to file into the locker room. They'd heard the news about Clark but had the same attitude as Cory. They wanted to win even more. Everyone had been inspired by the girls' efforts the day before. The Puff team was a real team, and knowing that made winning the icing on the cake.

"All right, girls," Jon's voice boomed over the loudspeaker. "The Deerfield team has a good record. They've only had two losses. Let's make it three today."

The team cheered, and even Cory started to get swept up in the excitement.

"There will be a short meeting on the field in ten minutes, so we'll—I mean *I'll*—meet you on the field then."

Cory noticed that all eyes were on her, waiting once again for her reaction. But she was still proud of the team, so instead of avoiding their glances, she decided to start a cheer. "Go Puffs, beat Deerfield," she yelled. She clapped her hands together and repeated her cry. Beth picked up the cue and was soon followed by Patti, Vicki, and the rest of the squad. Ten minutes later, the whole Puff team was ready and jogging out to the field to meet their rivals.

Attendance was the same as it had been at

the other Puff games. Deerfield had a smattering of fans that included a short, red-haired girl beating wildly on a bass drum. Cory felt a pang of disappointment when she reached the bench.

"I guess I thought things would be different after yesterday," Beth announced, reading Cory's mind.

"I was kind of hoping to meet our new, mysterious cheerleading squad," Vicki confessed.

"Well, I guess we'll just have to cheer ourselves on to victory," Cory said with a sigh. "I guess some things never change."

Without warning, the sounds of trumpets, drums, and shouts came from the other side of the field. The Puffs' fan club had arrived, and they were making their entrance with all the fanfare of a Fourth of July parade! Students were shaking pom-poms and carrying banners. Some band members had brought their instruments and were trying to blast out the school song. At least fifty of them trekked up to the home team's bleachers, shouting and cheering all the way. Then Cory noticed a group wearing pink, purple, and white uniforms marching in front of the Deerfield fans.

"It looks like our cheerleaders have shown up," Patti cried. As soon as she finished her statement there was a loud roar of laughter from the visitors' side. They were all pointing and giggling at the cheerleaders.

"Who are those girls?" Cory asked, squinting against the waning sun.

"They sure look big to me," Vicki said.

"Why, they're not girls at all!" Beth exclaimed.

"Isn't that Bob from the guys' football team?" Patti shouted.

Cory put up a hand to shield her eyes from the sun and looked across the field. "It's Clark," she cried, jumping to her feet. "He's dressed as the head cheerleader, leading a squad of football players!"

"She's right," Beth squealed, jumping up and down. By now the male cheerleaders had made their way past the Deerfield bench and were heading for their home bleachers right behind the girls' team.

"Puffs, Puffs, they're the best," Clark chanted through a large megaphone. "They can beat all the rest!"

Cory stood there with her mouth hanging open. She couldn't believe her eyes. Clark and the rest of his cheerleading squad were wearing dark purple knee-length pleated skirts, white bulky sweaters with purple paper emblems tacked onto the front, sneakers, and pink socks. All the girls on the team burst into laughter.

Without breaking rhythm, they filed in front of the Puff team, continuing their cheers. Cory continued to shake her head in disbelief until she noticed Clark marching right up to her. The next thing she knew, Clark had taken her into his arms, twirled her into a dip, and kissed her on the mouth. The kiss was long and gentle. Cory could barely respond, she was so shocked. He was acting as if there had been nothing wrong between them!

"I love you," he said when the embrace was over. "See you after the game."

Cory couldn't react fast enough. She felt like a robot who had just been short-circuited. Maybe she was dreaming. . . .

Jon blew the whistle loudly for the team to huddle, and Cory was snapped back to reality.

"The visitors are going to kick off, so we'll receive. Cory and Patti, try to gain us some territory running the ball back."

"Uh—sure, Coach," Cory answered before taking her place on the field. She stared at Clark, who motioned her to concentrate on the game.

The next minute the whistle blew, and Cory could see the ball coming directly at her. She could almost hear Clark giving her instructions. "Keep your eye on the ball. Follow it as it drops and hold your arms and elbows together like a basket. When you've caught it, secure it into position before you try to run, or it may fall out."

Everything went perfectly, and before Cory realized it she was heading down the field, past the thirty-yard line, the forty, the fifty, into their own territory to the thirty. The Deerfield girls were all grabbing for her flag, but the blockers were doing their jobs. Cory passed the ten-yard line and effortlessly bounded into the end zone for a touchdown! The fans and the team went wild. Cory felt invincible. She blew a kiss to Clark and then watched Patti kick the extra point.

The rest of the game was just as exciting.

Deerfield was quick and cunning, a team to be reckoned with. But every time Cory had a tough play, she heard Clark's voice coaching her inside her head. She hadn't realized until today how much she had learned from him. Cory had always thought of him as her boyfriend first and coach second. Now more than ever she wanted to talk to him, to set things right. She decided the best way to show him how she felt was to continue to prove to Clark that all his coaching had not fallen on deaf ears. When the final play of the game was completed and the Puffs had won 21–14, Clark rushed over to congratulate Cory.

"How about a little walk?" Clark suggested. "Right now I don't feel like a crowd."

"Anything you say, Coach." Cory couldn't stop smiling.

"I'm not your coach, I'm your cheerleader," Clark replied with a curtsy. They were quite a sight as they strolled away, Cory in her football uniform, and Clark dressed in a cheerleading skirt. He wrapped his arm around her shoulder and they wandered away from the field toward a small clump of trees at the end of the school grounds.

Cory held tight onto his waist and concentrated on the crisp, crunching sounds of leaves beneath their feet.

"There are so many things I want to say," Cory finally said, looking up at Clark.

"They're not important now," he said lightly, pressing his index finger to her lips.

"Yes, they are. I need to get them out before we can go on."

"All right, if you let me go first." Clark carefully sat Cory down on a twisted root of an old oak tree that had already lost most of its leaves. "As if you didn't know, I have quite an ego. I don't know if I'll ever get rid of it, but I'm hoping that I've learned not to let it get the best of me." Clark stood up and shuffled his feet through the small piles of leaves. "I was to blame for being late to the pancake breakfast, and I tried to put it off on you. When you came up with a successful football play, I should've realized that it didn't mean you doubted my abilities as a coach. But I was just so pigheaded that I felt threatened. Then of course there was the Battle of the Sexes." Clark stopped his pacing and sat next to Cory on the stump. He gently took her hand in his and continued. "But it was when I saw you at the bike races with Bryan that I knew I'd made a terrible mistake, and that I needed to do something or I'd lose not only my girlfriend, but a dear friend as well." He kissed her tenderly, and Cory felt all dizzy and warm.

"There's one other thing you should know about," Clark added.

"Lisa," Cory said.

"Yeah, Lisa. It seemed like every time you and I had a problem, she was there to pick up the pieces. She used her helpless charm to try to break us up."

"And it worked," Cory said, her face flushing with anger. "Every time I saw you two together, I just got angrier and more determined to prove I could do anything you could do."

"She was there to comfort me after the pancake breakfast," Clark explained. "Then she asked me to give her some private coaching so she could do better on the team. The more helpless she acted, the bigger I thought I was. That ego again! And when she showed up on our guys' night out, she made me wonder if I was wrong about us."

"Is—is that why you gave her your ring?" Cory asked hesitantly.

"I *never* gave her my ring," Clark stated emphatically.

"But I saw it around her neck," Cory answered firmly.

"Yes," Clark said grimly. "Jon noticed that Lisa was wearing it, too, and asked me about it. I never gave it to her." Clark took Cory's hands and held them tightly. "You've got to believe me."

"I do," Cory said after a moment. "But how—"

"Last night I confronted Lisa about the ring," Clark continued. "When you and I had our fight and I kicked you out of the game, you threw my ring onto the grass. Can't say I blame you," he added with a grin. "Anyway, I never saw you do that, but Lisa did. Before she ran onto the field, she scooped it up and started wearing it when I wasn't around. She was really desperate to make you think we were an item."

"I should've known better," Cory said. "I should have come to you right away."

"What's important is that we're together

now." Clark hugged Cory tightly to his chest. "That's why I want to put this in its proper place," he continued as he reached into a pocket underneath his sweater. He took out the ring, still on Cory's chain.

"May I ask you something first?" Cory said, stopping him from taking the ring off the chain and putting it on her finger.

"Sure," he whispered.

"Did you mean what you said when you kissed me before the game?"

"You mean, do I love you?"

"Yes," Cory said meekly.

"Yes, Cory, I love you. I really do. As a friend *and* a girlfriend."

"Then I don't need to wear your ring."

"What!" Clark said, looking stunned and confused.

"Well, it seems to me," Cory started to explain, "that this ring has caused us some trouble. Too many girls at school use these rings as something to hold on to their boyfriends with. That's not what I want. So I'd rather know you love me than wear your class ring. Maybe not wearing it will be a good reminder of what we can lose if we're not careful."

"Oh, Cory, you're the most beautiful, wonderful girl in the world," Clark said, hugging her tightly again.

Cory sighed and nestled her head against his shoulder. "And I love you, too."

SWEET DREAMS are fresh, fun and exciting—alive with the flavor of the contemporary teen scene—the joy and doubt of *first love*. If you've missed any SWEET DREAMS titles, then you're missing out on *your* kind of stories, written about people like *you*!

☐	26789	PAST PERFECT #134 Fran Michaels	$2.50
☐	26902	GEARED FOR ROMANCE #135 Shan Finney	$2.50
☐	26903	STAND BY FOR LOVE #136 Carol MacBain	$2.50
☐	26948	ROCKY ROMANCE #137 Sharon Dennis Wyeth	$2.50
☐	26949	HEART & SOUL #138 Janice Boies	$2.50
☐	27005	THE RIGHT COMBINATION #139 Jahnna Beecham	$2.50
☐	27061	LOVE DETOUR #140 Stefanie Curtis	$2.50
☐	27062	WINTER DREAMS #141 Barbara Conklin	$2.50
☐	27124	LIFEGUARD SUMMER #142 Jill Jarnow	$2.50
☐	27125	CRAZY FOR YOU #143 Jahnna Beecham	$2.50
☐	27174	PRICELESS LOVE #144 Laurie Lykken	$2.50
☐	27175	THIS TIME FOR REAL #145 Susan Gorman	$2.50
☐	27228	GIFTS FROM THE HEART #146 Joanne Simbal	$2.50
☐	27229	TRUST IN LOVE #147 Shan Finney	$2.50
☐	27275	RIDDLES OF LOVE #148 Judy Baer	$2.50
☐	27276	PRACTICE MAKES PERFECT #149 Jahnna Beecham	$2.50
☐	27357	SUMMER SECRETS #150 Susan Blake	$2.50
☐	27358	FORTUNES OF LOVE #151 Mary Schultz	$2.50
☐	27413	CROSS-COUNTRY MATCH #152 Ann Richards	$2.50
☐	27475	THE PERFECT CATCH #153 Laurie Lykken	$2.50

Prices and availability subject to change without notice.

- -

Bantam Books, Dept. SD, 414 East Golf Road, Des Plaines, IL 60016

Please send me the books I have checked above. I am enclosing $_____
(please add $2.00 to cover postage and handling). Send check or money order
—no cash or C.O.D.s please.

Mr/Ms_____

Address_____

City/State _____ Zip _____

SD—9/88

Please allow four to six weeks for delivery. This offer expires 3/89.

BANTAM
SHOP-AT-HOME
C·A·T·A·L·O·G

Special Offer
Buy a Bantam Book
for only 50¢.

Now you can order the exciting books you've been wanting to read straight from Bantam's latest catalog of hundreds of titles. *And* this special offer gives you the opportunity to purchase a Bantam book for only 50¢. Here's how:

By ordering any five books at the regular price per order, you can also choose any other single book listed (up to a $5.95 value) for only 50¢. Some restrictions do apply, so for further details send for Bantam's catalog of titles today.

Just send us your name and address and we'll send you Bantam Book's SHOP AT HOME CATALOG!